KEN LAMUG
MISCHIEF AND MAYHEM
BORN TO BE BAD

DANGER!!!

KEN LAMUG

MISCHIEF AND MAYHEM

BORN TO BE BAD

Katherine Tegen Books
An Imprint of HarperCollinsPublishers

Katherine Tegen Books and HarperAlley are imprints of HarperCollins Publishers.

Mischief and Mayhem: Born To Be Bad

For information address HarperCollins Children's Books, a division of HarperCollins Publishers,
195 Broadway, New York, NY 10007.
www.harpercollinschildrens.com
Library of Congress Control Number: 2020950992
ISBN 978-0-06-297076-3 (trade) — ISBN 978-0-06-297075-6 (pbk.)
21 22 23 24 25 GPS 10 9 8 7 6 5 4 3 2 1
❖
First Edition

THIS BOOK IS DEDICATED TO ALL THE KIDS WHO SIMPLY NEED TO LOOK INSIDE TO FIND A HERO.

AND TO SOPHIA, THANKS FOR TEAMING UP AND ALWAYS HAVING MY BACK. XO —K. L.

CHAPTER 1

THE GIRL NEXT DOOR AND HER FELINE FRIEND

BY DAY, SHE'S AN ORDINARY KID WITH AN ORDINARY CAT.
SHE DOES ORDINARY KID STUFF, LIKE GOING TO THE PARK . . .
WHOOPEE!
SPLASH!
READING LOTS OF BOOKS . . .
UGH!
PHYSICS
AND DOING COOL SCIENCE STUFF.
KAPOOF!

GIZMO ALSO DOES ORDINARY THINGS...
LIKE EATING...
NOM
NOM
NOM
MORE EATING...
CAKE
AND EVEN MORE EATING!
AND ALSO LOTS OF NAPPING.

GIZMO ALSO LIKES MESSING WITH DOGS.
HOWDY, FRIEND.
WOOF! WOOF!
FWIP!
AROOOOH!!
GOTCHA.
WHOA!
OUCH.
SPLAT!
THOUGH HE'S THE ONLY CAT WHO DOESN'T ALWAYS LAND ON HIS FEET.

BUT MILD-MANNERED MISSY HAS A WRINKLE IN HER SHIRT . . .
AWW . . . WHO WASHES THIS STUFF?
YOU?
A SMIRK IN HER SMILE . . .
THAT'S JUST CREEPY.
AND A STRUT IN HER WALK.
THIS IS CALLED "SWAGGER."
OH YEAH.

BECAUSE WHEN NO ONE IS AROUND . . .
IS ANYONE LOOKING?
NOPE!
PERFECTO!
HISTORY OF WALLPAP
VI SECRET DOOR
CLICK!
FWOOSH!
Let's Go!
TO UNDERGROUND LAIR

FWOOP!
SHWOOP!
CLIK!
FLAP!

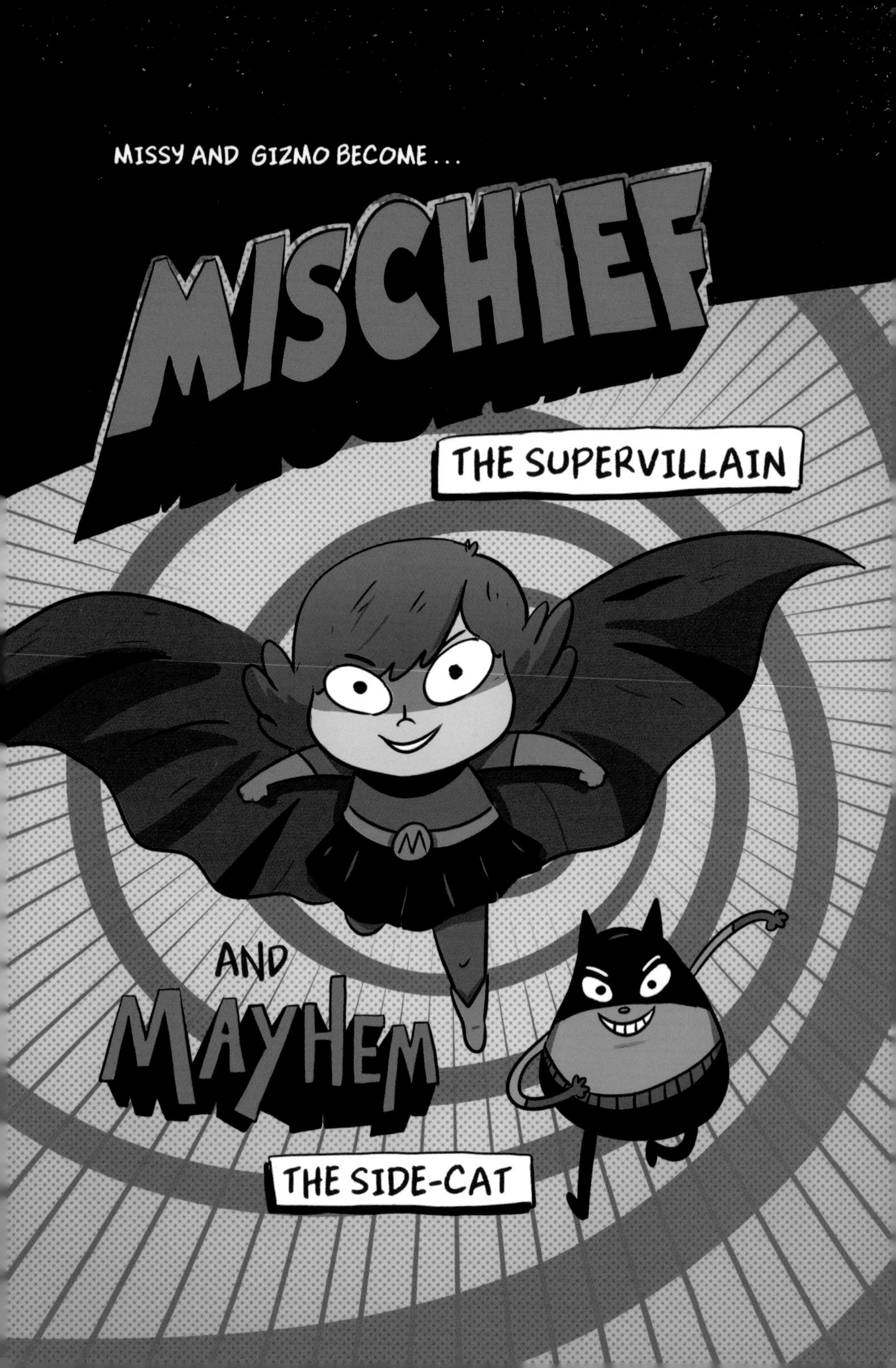
MISSY AND GIZMO BECOME . . .
MISCHIEF
THE SUPERVILLAIN
AND
MAYHEM
THE SIDE-CAT

I BET YOU'RE THINKING, "WHO WOULD WANT TO BE A SUPERVILLAIN?"
DUH. EVERYONE.
MAYBE NINE PEOPLE.
YOU THINK SUPERVILLAINS ARE BAD? THAT'S CALLED A MISNOMER.
TOPIC #29 VILLAINS NEED LOVE TOO.
YEP. IT'S NOT REAL.
BEING A SUPERVILLAIN IS SUPERFUN . . .
WE GET TO DO THINGS NO ONE ELSE CAN.
10,000 REASONS WHY IT'S COOL TO BE A SUPERVILLAIN!
3rd Edition

MISCHIEF'S SUPERVILLAIN PROFILE
STRONG, SMOOTH, AND STYLISH.
AWESOME HAIRSTYLE
SWEET MASK TO HIDE TRUE IDENTITY
FLASHY CAPE THAT FLAPS AGAINST THE WIND
POWER GLOVE WITH SECRET COMPARTMENT, BUILT-IN PEDOMETER AND PEW-PEW BLASTER
MISCHIEF-PATENTED ALL-IN-ONE TOOL BELT (COMFY FLEX-FIT, IMPORTANT)
AWESOME HIGH-TECH BOOTS (WATERPROOF) WITH MICROBOOSTERS BUILT INSIDE
✓ GRAPPLING HOOK
✓ FLASHLIGHT
✓ TOOTHPICK
✓ NIFTY GADGETS

MAYHEM'S PROFILE
DOES THIS MAKE MY BUTT LOOK BIG?
TRADEMARKED CAT MASK AND EAR PROTECTION
SNACK BELT WITH EXTRA POCKETS
PAW GLOVES
SLIM-FIT PANTS
RAISIN COOKIES
POTATO CHIPS
POTATO
JUICE BOX
APPLE

WHILE EVERYONE GOES TO BED...
TREVOR, GO TO BED!
COME ON, DO I HAVE TO?
IT'S TOO LATE FOR BAKING.
GO TO SLEEP!
MAX
NO FAIR!
FLOUR
FINISH THAT TOMORROW, YOUNG LADY.
AWWW, WE'RE ABOUT TO LIFT OFF!

SUPERVILLAINS STAY UP LATE, PAST THEIR BEDTIMES.
PILLOW FIGHT!
HI-YAH!
ICE CREAM AND POPCORN TIME!
OW! BRAIN FREEZE.
WE PLAY GAMES ALL NIGHT.
HIGH SCORE!
AND BUILD NEAT STUFF.
IT'S ALIVE!
HAR-HAR HAR-HAR!

AND WE SNEAK AROUND DARK PLACES WITHOUT BEING SEEN.
SHAKE
SHAKE
SHAKE
SPRAY PAINT
PSHHHT
Mischief was here!
A MASTERPIECE!
IT'S YOUR BEST WORK YET. THEY'LL SELL IT AT AUCTION.

SUPERVILLAINS ARE NOT SCARED OF THE DARK.
THE DARK IS SCARED OF US!
WEE-OOO!
WEE-OOO!
YIKES! IT'S THE POLICE!
RUN FOR IT!
HIDE HERE!
YEE-UCK! VILLAINS ARE NOT SUPPOSED TO GET MESSY.
TRASH
DRAT! WE LOST THEM AGAIN.
WE'RE NOT GOOD AT THIS. LET'S JUST GO GET BEAN BUNS.
TRASH

A SUPERVILLAIN DOES WHAT SHE WANTS AT THE MOVIES.
FUNNY
DRAMA
ACTION
AWARDS
THIS THEATER IS PACKED.
I CAN'T WAIT TO SEE THE MOVIE.
SNACKS
HOT DOGS
NACHO CHIPS
MOVE OVER!
SUPERVILLAINS COMING THROUGH!
BUMP
HEY!
HOW RUDE!
SODA POP
BUMP
BUMP!
SPLOOSH!
OOPSIE! SORRY.

YOU CAN KEEP THE DRINK. NO NEED TO THANK US.
SUPER-VILLAINS ARE THE WORST.
THE MOVIE'S STARTING.
FINALLY.
SNIFF. SNIFF. WHAT'S THAT SMELL?
IT'S NOT ME!
IT'S STINKING UP THE WHOLE PLACE.
IT'S HORRIBLE.
OVER THERE!

IT'S MY SPICY PICKLES! WANT SOME?
OOOH! YUMMY!
IT'S BETTER THAN POPCORN.
YUCK!
WHAT IS THAT ONE?
SNIFF SNIFF
PICKLED BLACK EGGS.
BARF!!
EW.
LET'S JUST WATCH.
STAY FAR AWAY
I HEARD ABOUT THIS PART. THE BAD GUY IS THE HERO'S DAD!

UH, DID WE DO SOMETHING WRONG?
USHER
MOVIES
YOU **RUINED** THE MOVIE!
USHER
OUCH.
BOINK
BOO! DON'T SPOIL THE ENDING.
EAT YER PICKLED STUFF SOMEWHERE ELSE!
SOME PEOPLE HAVE **NO** APPRECIATION.
I HEARD IT WAS A BAD MOVIE ANYWAY.

A SUPERVILLAIN DOESN'T NEED AN INVITATION TO PARTIES.
HELLOOO, LADIES.
UH, WHO INVITED HER?
NOT ME.
HERE'S OUR INVITATION.
THAT'S **FAKE.**
HAPPY BIRTHDAY
SO I GUESS YOU DON'T WANT YOUR GIFT?
YOU EVEN SPELLED MY NAME WRONG.
YOU ARE INVITED BY SOOZIN
REALLY? FOR ME?

IT'S A SPECIAL ONE.
VERY.
CAN I SEE IT?
FIRST, YOU HAVE TO SAY THE MAGIC WORD.
CAN I PLEASE SEE MY GIFT?
HERE YA GO!
FOOD FIGHT!
SHE DID SAY "PLEASE."
PIE SHOOTER 3000 XL

SPLAT!
SMOOSH!
SPLA-MOOSH!
THAT'S WHAT YOU GET FOR NOT INVITING ME.
HA-HA-HA!
RUUUNN!!!

AND BEST OF ALL, WHEN EVERYONE IS GONE...
WE GET TO EAT ALL THE DESSERTS.
CAKE, ICE CREAM, CANDIES . . . ALL THE FIXIN'S!
SUPERVILLAINS KNOW HOW TO PARTY!
POOL PARTY
FACE PAINTING
Dear Mischief and Mayhem,
You throw the BEST PARTIES!
Yours truly,
Mischief and Mayhem

BUT THE PATH TO SUPERVILLAINY WAS NOT ALWAYS EASY....
IT'S REALLY, REALLY HARD.
IT'S AN EMOTIONAL ROLLER COASTER.
YOU DON'T HAVE TO TELL ME, SISTER!

BEFORE SHE WAS A SUPERVILLAIN, MISSY WANTED TO BE A SUPERHERO.
HEY, THAT'S A SUPERSECRET STORY.
MELVIRA JUST CALLED ABOUT OUR NEXT MISSION.
ANOTHER ONE?
WE MUST BE THE HARDEST WORKING SUPERVILLAINS IN THE CITY.
LONG HOURS AND NO BENEFITS.
Hmmm. WE'LL CALL HER LATER.

FIRST WE HAVE A STORY TO TELL.
OH! THIS IS MY FAVE.
AN ORIGIN STORY OF EPIC PROPORTIONS!
MISCHIEF
THE TOTALLY AWESOME
SUPER-EPIC ORIGIN STORY
I CAN'T WAIT TO HEAR IT FOR THE 1,000TH TIME.
STRAP ON YOUR VELCRO GLOVES 'CUZ THIS IS HOW IT ALL STARTED.
ROLL THE TAPE!
DIRECTOR

SAVE THE CAT SAVE THE WORLD

IT ALL STARTED IN THE TOWN OF IDLEVILLE, A PLACE WHERE NOTHING INTERESTING HAPPENS.

THE TOWNSPEOPLE WERE ALWAYS BORED . . .
GOOD MORNIN', NEIGHBOR.
NOT GOOD, NOT BAD . . . JUST ANOTHER MORNIN'.
INDEED.
AHH. SAME OLD, SAME OLD.
WE'RE NOT THAT OLD.
THE ANIMALS WERE ALSO BORED . . .
I SHOULD BE CHASING YOU, BUT I JUST DON'T CARE.
I'M OFFENDED.
IN FACT, EVEN THE FLOWERS WERE BORED!
MEH.
MEH.

BUT ONE THING THAT EXCITED EVERYONE WAS THE FESTIVAL . . .
HERE THEY COME!
THE FLOATS LOOK FANTASTIC.
. . . CELEBRATING SUPERHEROES OF THE WORLD!
SUPER FESTIVAL
DAD, I WANT TO BE A HERO!
MAYBE ONE DAY.
SUPER FESTIVAL !!
SEE YOU NEXT YEAR!
BUT ONCE IT WAS OVER, THE BOREDOM OF IDLEVILLE RETURNED.

ONE SUMMER DAY, EVERYTHING CHANGED.
HONK! HONK!
HEAVENS TO BETSY!
LOOK OVER YONDER!
HONK!
YOU KIDS WILL LOVE OUR NEW PLACE!
CLANK
MOVE
IT'S SO . . . BLECH!
KA-CHUNK
WE'RE HERE!
SOLD
MOVE
SKREEEEK!

THE GO FAMILY HAD ARRIVED IN TOWN.
OUR NEW HOME!
ISN'T THIS EXCITING?
NEW NEIGHBOR-HOOD, NEW FACES, NEW THINGS TO DISCOVER.
R
AND DESPITE LIVING IN IDLEVILLE, THE GO FAMILY WAS ALWAYS ON THE GO!
QUIET DOWN, PLEASE! I CAN'T FOCUS.
GOTTA GO TO WORK, HON!
RAFI, PUT THAT DOWN!
SNOW-FLAKE'S GONNA GET YA!
DAD, LOOK! SNOWFLAKE IS GOING TO BE TRAUMA-TIZED!

THE GO FAMILY
THIS IS VINCENT, MISSY'S DAD. HE DESIGNS GREETING CARDS. HE USED TO HAVE A NORMAL SLEEPING SCHEDULE BUT NOW SURVIVES ON COFFEE AND CHEESY SNACKS.
AHHH . . . TRUE JOY COMES FROM FRESH ARABICA BEANS IN THE MORNING.
SLURP
OH! THAT WOULD MAKE A GOOD CARD.
DAD

HE ALSO COOKS AND CLEANS.
I GUESS THIS IS MY LIFE NOW.

THIS IS LUCY, MISSY'S MOM. SHE'S THE BREADWINNER AND ALWAYS BRINGS HOME THE BACON. ALTHOUGH MISSY HAS NEVER SEEN HER BRING HOME ANY BACON OR BREAD. SHE WORKS IN AN OFFICE AND STILL FINDS TIME TO DO THE BUDGET, TAXES, AND YOGA.
MOM
MOM, I DON'T SEE THE BACON.
THERE IS NO BACON.
ALSO, EVERY PLANT SHE TOUCHES SOMEHOW DISINTEGRATES.
SOB I DON'T GET IT!
I WATER THEM WITH LOVE AND TEARS, EVERY DAY.
WHOA!
NICE SUPERPOWER.

AND THERE'S MISSY'S ADOPTED BROTHER,
RAFI
STRAIGHT A'S AGAIN! THAT'S MY BOY.
OBVIOUSLY, HE GETS IT FROM ME.
SHOW-OFF! SCHOOL IS FOR SUCKERS!
A
OLD LADIES THINK I'M SUPERCUTE!
HE'S A DOLL.
ADORABLE!
RAFI'S ALSO PRETTY GOOD AT TAE KWON DO . . .
HI-YAH!
BOINK!
HEY!
AND VIDEO GAMES.
WOOH! BEAT YOU AGAIN.
STOP IT!

AND, OF COURSE, THE MOST IMPORTANT PERSON IN THIS STORY . . . MISSY!
SHE LOVES BUILDING STUFF.
MISSY THE INVENTOR
CLANG! CLANG!
UH . . . CAN YOU KEEP IT DOWN?
THE NOISE IS MELTING MY BRAIN!
YOU CAN'T KEEP GENIUS QUIET, DAD.
YOU SHOULD BE OUT, MAKING FRIENDS, GETTING FRESH AIR!
THAT'S WHY WE MOVED HERE. . . .
NO THANKS. EVERYTHING I NEED IS RIGHT HERE.
BRRRR
OKAY, HERE WE GO.
TEST #291!
CRACK-POP!
FLIP
IS IT SUPPOSED TO SOUND LIKE THAT?

BOOM
BUT SOMETIMES HER INVENTIONS DON'T EXACTLY WORK OUT.
THAT'S IT. I OFFICIALLY QUIT AS YOUR DAD.
IF THERE WAS ONE THING THE PEOPLE OF IDLEVILLE DIDN'T LIKE, IT WAS ALL OF MISSY'S NOISE.
IT INTERRUPTED THE IDLENESS OF THEIR SLEEPY TOWN.
BONK.
CLANG.
BZZZT.
KEEP DOWN THE RUCKUS. I CAN'T SLEEP!
SO SORRY!
IT'S DISTURBING MY TEATIME!

AND THEY ALL HATED MISSY'S PILE OF JUNK.
THIS IS NOT UP TO CODE!
WHAT A MESS.
MOM AND DAD HAD TO DO SOMETHING. ANYTHING!
MISSY, WE DISCUSSED IT, AND WE'VE MADE OUR DECISION.
YES, WE DID.
WAIT. WHAT DID WE DECIDE?
SHE'LL DO THE NEIGHBORS' CHORES. FIRST IMPRESSIONS LAST. AND SO FAR, EVERYONE THINKS WE'RE WEIRD!
NOT FAIR!
HA-HA. MISSY'S IN TROUBLE!

THIS IS WHO I AM— **AN INVENTOR!**
LISTEN TO YOUR MOTHER. NO IFs, ANDs, OR BUTs!
⋚SNICKER⋛ HA-HA. YOU SAID "BUTTS"!
IT'S NOT MY FAULT WE MOVED INTO THIS BORING TOWN.
MISSY, WHY NOT USE YOUR INVENTIONS TO DO SOME GOOD?
BE A HERO FOR THE NEIGHBORS. YOU KNOW THEY LIKE HEROES.
OK, FINE. I'LL SHOW THEM SOME MISSY GO GADGETS.
YOU SURE THIS IS A GOOD IDEA?
AT LEAST SHE'LL BE OUTSIDE.
GOOD POINT.

MISSY THE NEIGHBOR HELPER
YOUR DISHWASHER IS ALL FIXED UP MR. MACANNOY.
LET'S GIVE THIS A TRY.
BLEEP.
BOOP.
VRRM.
VRRRM.
VRRRM.
OH NO, TURN OFF!
KAPUT!
BAD DISHWASHER, BAD!

MISSY'S LANDSCAPING
DON'T WORRY, OLD LADY.
MY INVENTION WILL DO ALL THE WORK.
WOOF! WOOF!
YES! IT'S WORKING!
BZZZZTT
BZZZT
RUN, LITTLE BELLA! RUN!
OH, POOP!
BZZZZT
LOOK AT BELLA! YOU MISCHIEVOUS LITTLE GIRL!
SORRY, BELLA.

SUCH A CRUEL WORLD!
YOU TRY TO DO THE RIGHT THING, AND IT STILL GOES WRONG.
GET IT!
HA-HA-HA!
YOU CAN'T GET AWAY.
?
HERE, KITTY-KITTY.
WE'LL TOSS IT OVER THE BRIDGE!
NO. LET'S SHAVE IT FIRST! HA!
HISSS! GET AWAY!
HISSS, I SAID!
SWISH
LEAVE THIS TO ME, GUYS.
I'LL CLIMB THAT TREE. HEH-HEH.

MISSY THE CAT SAVER!
HEY, JERKS!
WHY DON'T YOU PICK ON SOMEONE YOUR OWN SIZE?
ONLY THING I SEE 'ROUND HERE IS A FLEA-SIZED HERO WANNABE.
SHOVE
JUST 'CUZ YOU'RE A GIRL, DON'T MEAN WE WON'T HURT YA.
WE'RE CERTIFIABLY NAUGHTY.
SEEMS LIKE YOUR BAD ATTITUDE NEEDS A LITTLE TRIMMING.
BZZZ
RUN!
WHAT THE HECK?
UH-OH! IT'S AFTER US!
CENSORED
BZZZT!

SINCE THAT DAY, MISSY AND GIZMO STUCK TOGETHER LIKE POTATOES AND GRAVY, OR SOCKS AND FEET.

BUT THE FATES CALLED UPON MISSY WHILE SHE WAS OUT SHOPPING...
SNACKS
RIC
FRESH BALUT
MARKET
POCK
HUH? WHAT'S THIS?
BE A HERO!
YOU ARE DESTINED FOR GREATNESS—
JOIN THE SUPERHERO BOOT CAMP
TIRED OF HIDING YOUR TRUE POTENTIAL?
IS EVERYONE IGNORING YOU?
WANT TO SAVE MORE THAN JUST CATS?
TIME TO LEVEL UP AND FULFILL YOUR DESTINY! APPLY TODAY!
*SCHOLARSHIPS AVAILABLE
*NOTE: YOU MUST HAVE SUPERPOWERS!
CALL 1-800-BE-A-HERO
A SIGN! MY DESTINY.
NEVER TRUST A DOG HOLDING A PAMPHLET.
BE A HERO
BESIDES, YOUR PARENTS WILL NEVER AGREE.
NO PROBLEMO. PAGES OF FORE-SHADOWING TELL ME THAT I'LL FIGURE IT OUT.

LATER THAT DAY . . .
WHAT? A BOOT CAMP?!
YES, A SCIENCE BOOT CAMP! PLEEAAASSSE, CAN I JOIN?
NO!
YOU ALWAYS SAID I NEEDED TO MAKE FRIENDS. THIS COULD BE HOW!
YOU CAN MAKE FRIENDS HERE.
IT'S NOT THE SAME.
THE KIDS HERE CAN'T RELATE TO MY AWESOMENESS.
THE BOOT CAMP KIDS ARE MORE LIKE ME.
YOU KNOW, THIS ISN'T THE FIRST TIME YOU TRIED TO DO SOMETHING NEW.
HERE WE GO AGAIN.

MISSY'S HOBBY CHECKLIST

EXTREME BUG COLLECTING
SHOW & TELL
FRIENDS
HOLY SMOKES, THAT'S HUGE . . .
WHAT-EVER THAT IS!
HIS NAME IS BIBI!
THIS IS BIBI'S FAMILY.
ROSS, SUE, OLLIE, MARK, TINA, RALPH . . .
AH!
CALL THE EXTERMINATORS!
AND THE BIG ONE BEHIND YOU IS RICK.
AAAHHH!

IF I DON'T DO THIS IT WILL RUIN MY LIFE! MY LIFE, DAD!
MY LIFE!
I'LL BE A ZOMBIE . . . WALKING THROUGH LIFE WITH NO PURPOSE.
HISSSSS
I'LL GET BUGGY EYES, PALE SKIN, TONGUE RASH . . .
YUMMY BRAIN MILK-SHAKE FLOAT
I'LL END UP LIVING WITH YOU UNTIL I'M 100 YEARS OLD!
GRANNY ZOMBIE MISSY
HOME SWEET HOME
WHAT?!
LIVE WITH US?
FOR A HUNDRED YEARS?!

Hmmm.
SHE HAS A POINT.
THAT'S A REALLY LONG TIME.
PLUS, IT'LL GIVE THE TOWN SOME PEACE AND QUIET.
OKAY.
FINE.
REALLY?
YES!
YES!
YOU'RE THE BEST.
YOU WON'T REGRET IT.

CHAPTER 3
THE BIG DAY AT BOOT CAMP
AFTER AN EXTREMELY LONG WAIT, MISSY FINALLY MAKES THE TRIP TO THE SUPERSECRET SUPERHERO BOOT CAMP.
SUPERHERO BOOT CAMP
BUS
COCK-A-DOODLE-DOO!
GOOD LUCK, LADY! DON'T EXPECT TO BE A HERO ON THE FIRST TRY!
BUS
GEE, THANKS FOR TIP, MISTER.
THAT GUY'S WEIRD.
OK, BREATHE.
FIRST IMPRESSIONS LAST. I GOT THIS.

RUSTLE
RUSTLE
ZIP
HUH?
BOINK!
FINALLY! WE ARRIVED!
THAT SUIT-CASE WAS CRAMPING MY STYLE.
WHAT THE HECK? DUDE, YOU CAN'T BE HERE.
WHY NOT? I'M YOUR SIDEKICK.
I'M NOT A SUPERHERO . . . YET.
YOU'LL GET US IN TROUBLE. LOOK . . .
NO PETS ALLOWED, ESPECIALLY CATS!
DON'T WORRY. I'M A MASTER OF STEALTH AND SNEAKINESS.
BESIDES, YOU HAVE A BIGGER PROBLEM!
WHAT?

YOU'RE AT A SUPERHERO BOOT CAMP, RIGHT?
YEAH?
YOU HAVE NO SUPERPOWERS.
ZIP. NADA. NONE!
ISN'T THAT KIND OF IMPORTANT?
I'M WORKING ON IT.
OKAY, IF YOU SAY SO. BUT . . .
SHHH. QUIET.
SOMEONE'S COMING. HIDE!
OKAY, OKAY!

AH! YES, YES. VELCOME, NEW RECRUIT.
YOU IS MISSY? BUT OF COURSE! AM IVAN. PLEASURE.
UH. HI, IVAN.
OH, IT TOOK MY BAG!
GRAB
WRRRP
BZZZ
WELCOME
TO SUPER
BOOT CAMP
HELPER BOT TAKE LUGGAGE. FOLLOW ME.
AS I SAY . . . WE BEST BOOT CAMP FOR WANNABE SUPER-PEOPLE. YOU **START TRAINING NOW.**
NOW?
I JUST GOT OFF AN 8-HOUR BUS RIDE.
CAN'T WE REST FOR A BIT?
THIS NO SPA DAY. ONLY CRASH COURSE!
FOLLOW ME. QUICKLY. YOU LATE.

WATER
THIS PLACE IS HUGE.
I WANNA SEE THE SPA.
MAIN SQUARE
CAFETERIA
SPA
CLASSROOMS
OBSTACLE COURSE
RESEARCH
WE GO TO MAIN SQUARE.
THIS TRAINING AREA. LOTS OF PAIN AND CRYING.
PAIN? THAT WASN'T IN THE AD.
WHAT'S THAT?
SUPER TOP SECRET BUILDING.
RESTRICTED AREA. **RECRUITS NOT ALLOWED!**
PROMISE YOU WON'T GO!
I PROMISE, MR. IVAN, SIR.

CLANG!
CLANG!
WE'RE LATE! LET'S RUN.
WHEW! AT LAST.
MAIN SQUARE
MEET NEW CAMPMATES . . .
AND YES, CAMP LEADER, GRU.
PABLO
DEENA
FISH
MELVIRA
BIGSBY
DERRICK
MISS GRU WELLING
SORRY, I UH . . .
LATE BUS, APOLOGIES . . .
THAT'S *MISS* GRU WELLING!
AND *YOU'RE* LATE!
NO EXCUSES. EVERYONE LINE UP!

I AM MISS GRU, YOUR CAPTAIN. FEARLESS LEADER. BIG HONCHO!
ZIP
AND IN THIS BOOT CAMP, THERE IS ONLY ONE ULTIMATE RULE: FOLLOW MY RULES! UNDERSTAND?
YES, MA'AM!
YOU WANT TO BE HEROES? YOU WILL WORK HARDER THAN YOU'VE EVER WORKED BEFORE.
SO MUCH WORK. SIGH
THERE WILL BE SWEAT. PAIN. SUFFERING.
OH. LOTS OF SUFFERING.

YOU WILL BE HELD TO THE HIGHEST STANDARDS . . . AND I WILL NOT TOLERATE ANY FUNNY BUSINESS!
NO JOKES.
YOU WILL DOUBT YOURSELF. YOU WILL CRY. YOU WILL ASK FOR MOMMY!
EVERY NIGHT, I DO.
AND AT THE END OF CAMP, YOU MUST PASS THE "ULTIMATE SUPERHERO TEST." THAT'S WHEN YOU GET YOUR OFFICIAL SUPERHERO NAME WRITTEN ON THIS . . .
CONGRATULATIONS
THE SUPERHERO CERTIFICATE
BRO . . . WHAT IS IT?
IT'S THE OFFICIAL SUPERHERO CERTIFICATE.
DUH, IT MEANS WE'RE REAL SUPERHEROES.
EXACTA-MUNDO.
YOU'RE CORRECT.
BIGSBY, WORK MORE ON THOSE BRAIN MUSCLES.

WAIT A SEC, I SMELL SOMETHING FISHY! SOMETHING IS NOT RIGHT.
SNIFF!
YOU MEAN, WRONG?
YOU!
ME? I SMELL FISHY?
QUIET!!!
I DIDN'T ASK FOR YOUR LIFE STORY.
AND WHAT MAKES YOU THINK YOU HAVE THE SKILLS TO BE IN MY BOOT CAMP?
I, UMM . . .
DON'T ANSWER THAT.
I DON'T WANT TO BE DISAPPOINTED THIS SOON.

YOU . . . YOU SMELL OF **FELINE.**
I HAVE A CAT— AT HOME, NOT HERE.
ACHOO!
I'M ALLERGIC TO CATS.
LOOK, I'M GETTING **HIVES!**
STATE YOUR NAME.
MISSY.
MISS WHAT?
MISSY.
THAT'S WHAT I'M ASKING, **MISS WHAT?**
THAT'S MY NAME.
YOUR NAME IS **WHAT?** THAT'S AN ODD NAME.
IT'S MISSY!
FINE. WHATEVER, **MISSY WHAT.** I'LL BE KEEPING AN EYE ON YOU. I DON'T TRUST CATS OR CAT PEOPLE.

SHE'S RUDE.
DID YOU SAY SOMETHING?
NOPE! I MEAN, UH . . .
I WAS JUST SAYING HOW HAPPY I AM TO BE HERE!
I'M WATCHING YOU. ALL OF YOU.
I HAVE EARS AND EYES BEHIND MY BACK!
I CAN SMELL TROUBLE A MILE AWAY!
NOW, EVERYONE, GIVE ME ONE THOUSAND LAPS!
GO! GO! GO!! GOOO!!!
YES, MA'AM!

NO PAIN, NO GAIN!
IS IT LEG DAY? I HATE RUNNING!
NOBODY LOVES RUNNING.
I LOVE TO RUN! IT'S HOW I DEAL WITH MY ANXIETY.
OH MY GOSH. I ALREADY HAVE ROCKS AND DIRT IN MY SHOES.
GERMS, GERMS EVERY-WHERE!
HUFF-HUFF. OH NO. I'M GETTING LEFT BEHIND.
I'M SO OUT OF SHAPE.
WHOOPS!
WHOA!
TRIP
OW!
UGH. I ALREADY HATE THIS PLACE.

YOU OKAY THERE?
JUST A LITTLE NICK.
OW.
HERE, LET ME FIX THAT.
NAME'S MELVIRA.
MISSY. NICE TO MEET YA.
DON'T WORRY ABOUT TRYING TO OUTRUN THEM.
THEY ALWAYS TRY TO SHOW OFF ON THE FIRST DAY.
IT'S THE SAME AT EVERY BOOT CAMP.
OH, YOU'VE BEEN TO OTHERS?
LET'S JUST SAY IT'S NOT MY FIRST RODEO.
TELL YOU WHAT, I KNOW A SHORTCUT IF YOU PROMISE NOT TO TELL.
MY LIPS ARE SEALED. LET'S DO THIS!

THE PLOT THICKENS
LATER THAT NIGHT . . . A SINISTER PLAN IS AFOOT!
HELLO, READER!
IT TOOK YOU AWHILE TO GET TO MY PART, BUT HERE WE ARE!
MELVIRA
MASTER OF DISGUISE AT YOUR SERVICE.
CLAW
BIRD SIDEKICK
YOU MIGHT THINK I'M A GOODY TWO-SHOES HERO WANNABE . . . BUT I AM IN FACT A VILLAIN!
BAWK!
CLAW STOLE THIS MAP. X MARKS THE SPOT— THE LOCATION OF THE TOP SECRET STORAGE BUNKER IS SOMEWHERE HERE IN BOOT CAMP!
BOOT CAMP MAP
TOP SECRET STORAGE BUNKER

AND DEEP IN THE BUNKER, PROTECTED BY A HIGH-TECH SECURITY SYSTEM, IS WHERE THEY HAVE THE BLUEPRINTS FOR THE ULTIMATE WEAPON.
MAP
PLAN
BUNKER
MORE MAPS
BAWK!
YOU'RE RIGHT, CLAW. WITH THE BLUEPRINTS, WE CAN BUILD THE ULTIMATE WEAPON THAT WILL STOP ALL HEROES FOREVER!
HEROES THINK THEY'RE BETTER THAN US . . . BUT THEY'RE NOTHING WITHOUT POWERS!
SUPERHERO
MINUS
POWER
EQUALS SUPERDUD!
BAWK!
ALL WE NEED TO DO IS FIND THE BUNKER, BREAK IN, AND STEAL THE BLUEPRINTS!
HA-HA-HA-HA!

CHAPTER 4

NO PAIN, NO GAIN. LET'S GO TRAIN!

AT BOOT CAMP, YOU NEVER STOP RUNNING. . . .
FASTER! RUN! RUN! RUN!
MY PANTS!
LAPS TO GO 99,999
ZZZ
I NEED TO BRUSH MY TEETH FIRST! OH NO, I FORGOT MY SANITIZER.
I'M WITH YOU ON THAT ONE, DUDE!
HUH?
IS SHE SLEEP-WALKING?
ZZZ
HEY, WAKE UP! SUPERHEROES DO NOT SLEEPWALK!
YAAHHH!
I'M UP!
I'M UP!

I EXPECT EVERYONE TO WAKE UP AT THIS TIME EVERY DAY!
PSST.
HERE, DRINK THIS.
GLUG
GLUG
GLUG
YOWZA! I FEEL ENERGIZED.
IT'S MY SPECIAL JOLT DRINK.
IT COULD WAKE UP A SLEEPING ELEPHANT.
THAT'S EXACTLY WHAT I NEED.
I FEEL LIKE I COULD RUN A HUNDRED MILES!

ON SOME DAYS, YOU RUN UP HILLS . . .
HUFF-HUFF
MAYBE I CAN RUN ONE MILE.
YOU RUN DOWN HILLS . . .
AHHH! ACK!
I SWALLOWED A BUG.
AND YOU LEAP OVER OBSTACLES.
ARE WE TRAINING TO RUN AWAY?
THEY'RE MORE SCARED OF YOU THAN YOU ARE OF THEM!
WORST DAY EVER!

THERE'S ALSO CLIMBING . . .
MY ARMS ARE HURTING.
AND FALLING. LOTS AND LOTS OF FALLING.
WHOA!
HELP!
AIIIEEE!
OOOF!
MOMMY!

AND WHEN THEY'RE NOT TRAINING, THE RECRUITS RELAX AND PLAY DURING A MUCH-NEEDED BREAK. . . .
NOW, THIS IS THE LIFE. JUST US AND MOTHER NATURE.
IT'D BE BETTER IF IT WASN'T SO HOT.
JUMP IN, IT'S NICE.
UH, NO. THAT WATER IS AN ECOSYSTEM OF ICKY STUFF!
HA-HA!
I THINK YOU NEED TO COOL OFF.
SPLASH
WHOA! WHAT THE HECK, MAN?
AH! I CAN'T SWIM! HELP ME!
DUDE, IT'S NOT DEEP.

NO HORSING PLAY. SAFETY FIRST! BUT ALSO, HAVE FUN!
HEY DEENA, WANT TO JOIN ME?
I JUST GOT SETTLED. ENJOYING THIS NICE SUN.
WANNA SIT?
I'M CAKED WITH FOUR LAYERS OF SPF-300 SUNSCREEN. NO TANNING FOR ME.
SUIT YOURSELF.
WHAT ABOUT YOU? WHAT ARE YOU DOING?
OH HEY, JUST SOME CARTOG-RAPHY.
YOU'RE INTO MAPS, HUH? THAT'S FUN!
YUP!

HEY! WANT TO HEAR A MAP JOKE? WHICH IS SMARTER, LONGITUDE OR LATITUDE?
HUH? UMMM... I GIVE UP.
LONGITUDE! BECAUSE IT HAS 360 DEGREES. HA-HA-HA!
OHHH, LIKE COLLEGE DEGREES! FUNNY!
WANT TO JOIN ME? I HAVE LOTS OF STUFF TO DO!
I WILL UNDER TWO CONDITIONS.
WE VISIT THE AREAS I MARKED ON THE MAP, AND YOU STOP TELLING JOKES.
YOU'VE GOT A DEAL, PARTNER!
SECRET BUNKER

MELVIRA ONLY JOINED MISSY SO SHE COULD LOOK FOR THE STORAGE BUNKER, BUT THAT DIDN'T MEAN THEY DIDN'T HAVE FUN, TOO.

YUM TIME
TOP SECRET STORAGE BUNKER
I CAN'T REMEMBER THE LAST TIME I HAD THIS MUCH FUN.
SAME! BUT I'M STARVING.
WE SHOULD HEAD BACK.

BACK AT CAMP . . .
ONE THING'S FOR SURE, **FOOD HERE IS GOOD!**
THE TEA CALMS ME DOWN.
THIS IS A **FEAST**.
YUP.
NOM
NOM
HEY, I'VE BEEN WONDERING . . .
WHAT'S THAT?
WITH ALL THIS BOOT CAMP TRAINING, HOW COME WE HAVEN'T DONE ANY SUPERHERO STUFF YET?

THAT'S EASY. MISS GRU WANTS TO SEE WHO'S THE TOUGHEST.
DUDE!
I'M THE TOUGHEST!
AND STRONGEST.
UH . . . CAN YOU KEEP IT DOWN?
RIGHT NOW, YOUR UNDERARM SMELL IS WHAT'S MOST POWERFUL.
BIGSBY, YOU'RE NOT THAT STRONG.
I ACCEPT YOUR CHALLENGE. HOW ABOUT A
SUPERPOWER SHOW-OFF!

I'M BIGSBY, AND MY POWER IS SUPERSTRENGTH!
FLIP!
AIIIEEE! ARE YOU CRAZY?
BIGSBY SMALLS
RECRUIT ID: 0209
POWERS: SUPERSTRENGTH
SUPERMOVE: CANNONBALL
WEAKNESS: NAP TIME, GETS CONFUSED EASILY
IT'S MY TURN.
I'M EXCHANGE STUDENT GOLDY. I CAN TALK TO SEA CREATURES AND BLOW BUBBLES!
GOLDY
RECRUIT ID: 0213
POWERS: SWIMMING, TALKING TO SEA ANIMALS
SUPERMOVE: FISH SUMMONING
WEAKNESS: OPEN AIR
I GUESS I'M NOT REALLY USEFUL ABOVE WATER.

I'M DERRICK,
AND I'M ICY!
I'M DEENA,
AND I'M FLAMING HOT!
DERRICK DUO
RECRUIT ID: 0211
POWERS: WATER AND ICE
SUPERMOVE: ICE CUBES
WEAKNESS: SUMMERTIME & HOT POCKETS
DEENA DUO
RECRUIT ID: 0210
POWERS: EXTREME HEAT
SUPERMOVE: FIREBALL
WEAKNESS: WATER
WITH DERRICK AND DEENA, WE CAN HAVE A PROPER BARBECUE.
I'LL BRING THE MARSHMALLOWS, YOU BRING THE LEMONADE.

PABLO PACE
RECRUIT ID: 0214
POWERS: SUPERSPEED
SUPERMOVE: SKIP LINES, SPEED SHOVE
WEAKNESS: STOPLIGHTS, CLUMSINESS
PABLO HERE... I'M SUPERSONIC SPEEDY.
SWOOOSH!
THAT'S HANDY AT THE COUNTY FAIR. NO MORE LINES.
I'M MELVIRA AND I CAN TRANSFORM!
ZOOP-ZIP-ZWOOSH!
MAIL
MELVIRA HOTDOG
MELVIRA MAILBOX
MELVIRA MONSTER
MELVIRA HEEL
RECRUIT ID: 0215
POWERS: DISGUISE AND TRANSFORM (BUT CAN'T COPY POWERS OR ABILITIES)
SUPERMOVE: MIND TRICKS
WEAKNESS: TICKLES
WHOA, THAT'S RADICAL.
MELVIRA BIGSBY

MISSY GO
RECRUIT ID: 0216
POWERS: SCIENCE & BUILDING STUFF
SUPERMOVE: LIMITLESS IMAGINATION
WEAKNESS: BOREDOM, PHYSICAL ACTIVITY
I'M MISSY, AND I HAVE THE POWER OF SCIENCE!
CHECK IT OUT: SOAPY SUD BLASTER!
GRABBY ARM EXTENDER!
FIDGET SPINNER BOOMERANG!
BUILDING STUFF IS NOT A SUPERPOWER.
HA-HA-HA-HA!
OF COURSE IT IS!
I'VE GOT THE BRAINS, SKILLS, AND DETERMINATION!

WELL, WE'RE ALL SORT OF SMART OR WE WOULDN'T BE HERE.
WE ARE?
BUT I'M **REALLY SMART**. LOOK AT THIS STUFF.
DON'T YOU HAVE ANY **SPECIAL ABILITY?**
LIKE WHAT?
HOW TO GET SUPERPOWERS
POWERS FROM INSECT BITES
WERE YOU BITTEN BY A MUTANT SPIDER AND CAN SHOOT SPIDER WEBS?
PEW. PEW.
YUCK.
SPIDERS CREEP ME OUT.
PSSSHHH

POWERS FROM ALIEN ORIGINS
DID YOU CRASH-LAND IN A SPACE POD WHEN YOU WERE A BABY?
AND NOW YOU CAN FLY AND GET POWER FROM THE SUN?
I FELL OUT OF MY BED.
PLOP!
POWERS FROM SCIENCE EXPERIMENT
WERE YOU IN A FAILED EXPERIMENT THAT TURNED YOU INTO AN ANGRY GREEN MONSTER?
HELP!
HMM. THIS VEIN POPS WHEN I GET FRUSTRATED.
CAN YOU SHOOT LASER BEAMS OUT OF YOUR EYES?
SHOOM!!
I CAN SQUIRT WATER OUT OF MY NOSE!

WELL, IF YOU **DON'T** HAVE SUPERPOWERS, YOU **CAN'T** BE A SUPERHERO.
IT TOTALLY SAYS SO IN THE RULEBOOK.
SEE?
GULP!
AND THE PENALTY FOR LYING IS . . .
. . . YOU GET **KICKED OUT OF BOOT CAMP.**
I DIDN'T LIE. **I SWEAR!**
I JOINED JUST LIKE YOU GUYS, FAIR AND SQUARE.
THERE'S ONLY ONE WAY TO FIND OUT.
LET'S GO ASK . . .

HEY! TAKE IT EASY!!
I KNOW FOR A FACT THAT MISS GRU HAD A VERY GOOD REASON FOR ACCEPTING MISSY.
ARE YOU SAYING YOU **KNOW BETTER** THAN HER?
ARE YOU GUYS GOING TO WALK OVER TO HER OFFICE AND QUESTION HER ABILITY TO RUN THE CAMP?
WELL . . . **NO.**
YEAH, NOT A GOOD IDEA.

BUT IT DOESN'T MEAN WE HAVE TO LIKE IT. HMPH!
BOGUS, AND I THOUGHT YOU WERE COOL.
SHE SHOULDN'T BE HERE.
HMPH!
MUST
WELL . . .
I MIGHT AS WELL PACK IT UP.
THEY'RE **NOT** GOING TO TELL.
THEY'RE TOO SCARED OF MISS GRU.

I'VE SEEN THOSE FACES BEFORE.
THEY DON'T LIKE ME.
I THOUGHT THE KIDS HERE WOULD BE DIFFERENT.
I THOUGHT I COULD MAKE FRIENDS. BUT IT ALWAYS ENDS THE SAME WAY.
BUT YOU DID MAKE A FRIEND.

SUPERHERO CLASS
MISSY COULDN'T DWELL ON HER INSECURITIES FOR LONG. CLASSES HAD STARTED AND THE TRAINING WAS INTENSE.
DEFEATING HENCHMEN 101
HENCHMAN
CLUMSY AND EVIL, AND THEY NEVER STOP COMING—MEET THE HENCHMEN!
HEY! THERE ARE HENCH-GIRLS TOO, YA KNOW.
ENCHMAN
I CAN STOP THEM WITH THIS.
OH, THIS WILL BE GOOD.
KA-POW!!
HENCHMAN
AAAEEIIII!!
CAN I BE THE HERO NOW?

HERO CATCHPHRASES AND POSES 101

AT THE END OF EACH DAY, WHEN EVERYONE'S ASLEEP, MISSY SNEAKS OFF TO THE SCIENCE WORKSHOP.
I MIGHT NOT HAVE POWERS, BUT I CAN STILL BE A HERO. I'M JUST GONNA HAVE TO WORK EXTRA HARD.
RIGHT. AND I'M HERE TO GIVE FULL EMOTIONAL SUPPORT.
HMMM. I WONDER WHAT SHE'S UP TO?
SCIENCE & TECHNOLOGY
I'LL SHOW EVERYONE I BELONG.
POWER SUIT PLAN #5
STRENGTH
RZ-30 SOURCE
SHE'LL NEED TO BUILD QUICKLY BECAUSE THE FINAL SUPERHERO TEST IS COMING SOON.

CHAPTER 5
LIAR! LIAR!
STUFF ON FIRE!
FINISHED JUST IN TIME!
I DID IT!
THE SUIT IS READY.
SUPERHERO TEST, HERE I COME!
POPCORN READY, FLIP THAT SWITCH!
BEEP!
IT WORKS! WE'RE IN BUSINESS.
SUPERSTRENGTH!
SUPER-PUNCH!
RIP!
OH NO! I THINK THERE'S SOMETHING WRONG WITH THE SUIT.
BZZZT!
POOF

YIKES!
FIRE!
FWOOM!
WOOOSSHHH
GRRR! WHY ME?!
I HAVE AN IDEA.
LET'S FORGET THIS WHOLE THING, GO HOME, AND EAT ICE CREAM AND PICKLED GARLIC!
WE DON'T NEED TO BE HEROES.
DON'T YOU GET IT?
ALL MY LIFE I'VE TRIED BEING NORMAL.
I FOLLOWED THE RULES, TRIED TO FIT IN.
BUT IT ALWAYS ENDS THE SAME.
ME, ALONE.

I JUST WANT TO BE ALLOWED TO BE ME.
FISH SWIM. BIRDS FLY. I CREATE.
THIS IS WHO I AM.
THIS IS WHAT I DO.
BUT I . . .
JUST GO, GIZMO. I NEED TO FIGURE THIS OUT.

UNSURE HOW TO HELP MISSY, GIZMO DID WHAT GIZMO DOES BEST . . . HAVE FUN!
AT THE POOL . . .
CANNONBALL!
SPLASH!
AT THE PLAYGROUND . . .
MY BACKHAND NEEDS WORK.
POW
POP
AND AT THE BUFFET.
YUMMY.
EVEN AT THE GIFT SHOP.
BETTER GET SOME SOUVENIRS . . .

THERE HE IS!!
HE MADE THE POOL DIRTY!
HE HIT MY EYE WITH A BALL!
AND HE DID THIS!
YIKES! THAT'S MY CUE TO RUN!
GET HIM!!!
GIFTS
YOU HAVE ME CONFUSED WITH ANOTHER CAT.

MEANWHILE, BACK AT THE LAB . . .
MISSY?
ARE YOU OK?
SURE. YEAH.
NO! I'M DOOMED!
DOOMED, YA HEAR ME?! I LIED TO EVERYONE.
I'M A BIG FRAUD.
I'LL RETURN HOME EMBARRASSED AND ASHAMED!
I THOUGHT I WAS DESTINED TO BE A SUPERHERO, BUT I WAS JUST LYING TO MYSELF.

MISSY . . . YOU CAN'T GIVE UP NOW. THIS IS JUST A BUMP ON YOUR ROAD TO GREATNESS.
WHAT ARE YOU EVEN TALKING ABOUT?
YOU'RE SMART.
YOU CAN DO MORE COMPLEX SCIENCE THAN ANYONE I KNOW.
THAT'S BETTER THAN ANY SUPERPOWER.
YOU THINK SO?
I KNOW SO.
SUPERPOWERS ARE OVERRATED!
PICK YOURSELF UP AND SHOW EVERYONE WHAT YOU CAN DO WITH BRAINPOWER!
I WOULD, BUT I'M MISSING A PART TO GET MY POWER SUIT WORKING.

Hmmm.
I MIGHT HAVE AN IDEA.
BUT HOW FAR ARE YOU WILLING TO GO TO BE A HERO . . . TO FULFILL YOUR DESTINY?
I'LL DO ANYTHING.
THERE'S A PLACE WHERE THEY KEEP ALL THE HIGH-TECH PARTS.
WHERE?
THE TOP SECRET STORAGE BUNKER!

TOP SECRET STORAGE BUNKER. THIS ONE!
THE TOP SECRET STORAGE BUNKER
WHEW! ACCORDING TO MY MAP, THIS IS IT!
ARE YOU SURE WE CAN BE HERE?
DON'T BE SILLY. OF COURSE WE CAN!
WARNING
I DUNNO . . . MAYBE IT'S THE ROBOT GUARDS . . .
OR THE TRAPS . . .
SECRET STORAGE BUNKER
OR MAYBE IT'S JUST THAT SIGN.
RESTRICTED AREA AUTHORIZED PERSONNEL ONLY
BUT I DON'T THINK WE'RE ALLOWED IN.
THIS IS LEGIT!
BESIDES, WE'RE JUST "BORROWING."
LOOK, DO YOU WANT THIS OR NOT?
YES, I DO!

TIME TO SHOW YOUR CHOPS. THE SUPERHERO TEST IS STARTING SOON.
CAN YOU BREAK THE CODE TO GET IN THIS DOOR?
LOOKS LIKE A PUZZLE CODE.
AHA! EASY PEASY. ALL I HAVE TO DO IS . . .
BOOP! BEEP!
I COULDN'T FIGURE THAT OUT.
WELCOME!
WHOA. NEAT.
A5
DID YOU KNOW THAT A LONG TIME AGO . . .

THERE WAS A SCIENTIST WHO WORKED HERE.
HE INVENTED GADGETS AND SUITS FOR THE HEROES.
SOME SAY HE BECAME MAD WITH POWER...
HA HA HA HA HA HA HA
OTHERS SAY THE COUNCIL OF HEROES BECAME JEALOUS.

EITHER WAY, HE WAS BANISHED, NEVER TO BE HEARD FROM AGAIN.
ALL HIS INVENTIONS AND EXPERIMENTS WERE TAKEN AWAY . . .
STORAGE BUNKER
TOP SECRE
TOP SECRET
AND HIDDEN IN SECRET LOCATIONS.
THAT'S WHY HEROES AREN'T ALLOWED TO RELY ON GADGETS.

WOW, THAT'S SAD. WE COULD DO SO MUCH WITH ALL THESE TOOLS AND PARTS.
I BET WE COULD TAKE OVER THE WORLD.
X1
THERE! IT'S IN THAT VAULT.
IT NEEDS A FACE SCAN . . . OF MISS GRU WELLING.
WE CAN'T UNLOCK THIS!
FACE SCAN GRU WELLING
NOT TO WORRY! THAT'S MY SPECIALTY!
ZOOP
ZIP
ZOOP
ZOOP
ZIP
ZWOOSH!
TA-DA!
I AM GRU! GIVE ME A THOUSAND LAPS!
HA! YOU EVEN SOUND LIKE HER.

LET'S TRY THIS.
BZZT.
SCAN
BRRRRP. CHECKING FACE . . .
BOOP. BOOP. FACE SCAN COMPLETE.
WELCOME, GRU WELLING.
OK.
BZZZTTTT!
IT WORKED!
WOW! LOOK AT THESE. . . . I'M GEEKING OUT!

I THINK I CAN FIND WHAT I NEED HERE.
TAKE YOUR TIME. I'LL JUST POKE AROUND.
OMG! THE BLUEPRINTS!
HA-HA HA!
I'M A GENIUS! THIS IS THE BEGINNING OF THE END FOR HEROES . . .
RUMBLE! RUMBLE!
UH-OH! WHAT'S THAT?
MELVIRA, I FOUND THE MISSING PART!
HUH?
PARTS
CAPACITOR
ALERT!
ALERT!
ALERT!
ALERT!

UH, MELVIRA . . .
RUN!
IT'S A SECURITY ROBOT. DID YOU TRIP AN ALARM?!
ALARM!
NO! I SWEAR.
CRASH!
SMASH!
SEARCH AND DESTROY.
I'M TOO YOUNG TO DIE!
?
I HAVE AN IDEA.
HEY, ROBOT! I AM GRU, AND I COMMAND YOU TO STOP!
GRU?

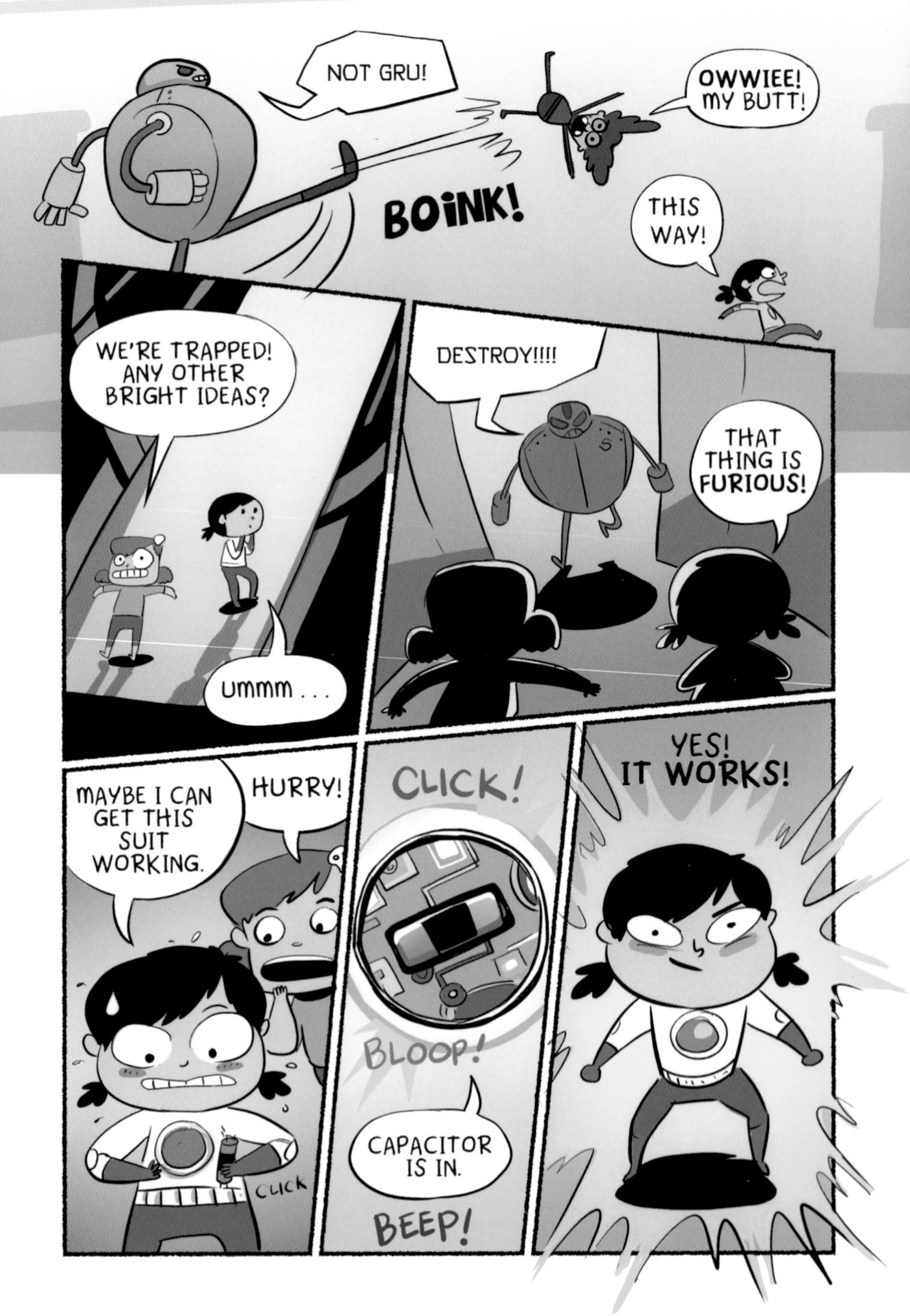
NOT GRU!
OWWIEE! MY BUTT!
BOINK!
THIS WAY!
WE'RE TRAPPED! ANY OTHER BRIGHT IDEAS?
UMMM . . .
DESTROY!!!!
THAT THING IS FURIOUS!
MAYBE I CAN GET THIS SUIT WORKING.
HURRY!
CLICK
CLICK!
BLOOP!
CAPACITOR IS IN.
BEEP!
YES! IT WORKS!

TAKE THIS!
POWER SUIT STICKY SLUDGE!
SPLOOCH!
WOOSH!
YOU MISSED!
SORRY! I HAVE BAD AIM.
KEEP TRYING!
SPLOOCH!
GOT HIM!
SPLAT!
ERROR. VISION DISABLED.
ERROR!
ERROR!
SMASH!
SMASH!
IT'S OUT OF CONTROL!

SMASH!
ERROR!!!!
THAT'S ONE ANGRY ROBOT!
THANKS FOR THE EXIT, ROBOT!
AMAZING WORK, MISSY. YOU HAVE A REAL TALENT FOR THIS.
THAT WAS EXCITING.
FIST-BUMP!
OH YEAH!
OH NO, WE'RE GOING TO MISS THE TEST.
GO! I'LL MEET YOU DOWN THERE!
YOU GOT THIS, MISSY!
THANKS, I OWE YOU!

PSSST!
ARE YOU THERE?
BAWK! BAWK!
HELLO, MY BIRD-BRAINED FRIEND.
HERE, TAKE THE BLUEPRINTS.
BWA-HA-HA!
THAT WAS EASIER THAN I EXPECTED.
THANKS TO MISSY.
BAWK! BAWK! BAWK!
YOU'RE RIGHT. SHE'S PRETTY HANDY.
SHE COULD BE A STRONG ALLY.
IT'S ALL COMING TOGETHER.
HIGH-FIVE!
BAWK!

CHAPTER 6
THE SUPERPOWER SHOW-DOWN!
CLANG!
CLANG!
RECRUITS, LINE UP!
YOU MUST PROVE YOUR WORTH TO BE A SUPERHERO. YOU MUST SHOW CONTROL OVER YOUR POWERS AND TRIUMPH OVER OBSTACLES . . .
AND CLAIM YOUR HERO NAMES.
WHERE ARE MISSY AND MELVIRA?
I DUNNO, BRO.
MAYBE THEY QUIT?
THEY BETTER SHOW UP SOON.

RECRUITS WILL TACKLE OBSTACLES TAILORED TO THEIR ABILITIES
CAPTURE THE FLAG AND WIN THE CHALLENGE.
LET'S GO!
A BATTLE OF STRENGTH!
HMPH!
GRAB
DUDE, THIS GUY IS STRONG!
SMACK!
OUCH!
NOW WE'RE HAVING FUN!
A BATTLE OF SPEED!
COME HERE, YA LITTLE BUGGER!
ZOOM!

YIKES! I'M GONNA NEED MOISTURIZER AFTER THIS.
PSSHHH!!
WHOA! TOO CLOSE.
WHY DID IT HAVE TO BE AN ICE MONSTER?
ROAR!
COME ON, WORK . . .
PFFFT.
WORK!
WHOA!
SUCH A COLD PERSONALITY!
SMASH!

EACH RECRUIT REMEMBERED A MOMENT IN TRAINING WHERE THEY FELT DEFEATED, AND USED THAT STRENGTH TO FIGHT ON AND WIN THE CHALLENGE.
MAIN SQUARE
BUT WILL MISSY MAKE IT IN TIME?

LATER . . .
SURPRISING. EVERYONE PASSED TEST. BUT . . . ALL NEED HOSPITAL, YES?
WAIT! MISSY IS MISSING!
HERE! READY TO GO!
SHE ARRIVES! SHE CAN TAKE TEST! WHEW
Hmmm. LATE AGAIN!
BOOM! BOOM! BOOM!
WHAT IS THAT SOUND?
SOUNDS BIG, YES?

ROBOT VS EVERYONE!
SECURITY ROBOT IS MALFUNCTION!
OUCHIE!
SEARCH! DESTROY!
IT'S GONE CRAZY!
HEROES, STOP THAT ROBOT!
IT'S NOT WORKING.
KEEP TRYING.
DON'T WORRY, GUYS.
I HAVE SHARK POWER!
SHARK?!
ARE YOU NUTS? WHERE'D YOU GET A SHARK!?
BAD SHARK! FIGHT ROBOT, NOT FRIENDS!
SMASH!

WHAT'S GOING ON? IS THE TEST OVER?
THE ROBOT GUARD'S GONE CUCKOO!
LET ME GO, YOU RUSTED OLD JUNK.
DESTROY!
BONK!
OOFF!
WE'RE GONERS!
DO SOMETHING, MISSY!
YOU STOPPED IT BEFORE!
RIGHT. TIME TO PUT THE POWER SUIT TO THE TEST.
THWACK!
HI-YAH! STICKY SLUDGE!
IT KNOWS THAT TRICK ALREADY!
OH YEAH?!
TRY MY TANGLE WIRES!

THERE'S A SWITCH. FIND IT!
GRRR. DESTROY!
GO, MISSY! WE'LL TRY TO HOLD IT DOWN.
AHA!
WHY DIDN'T I SEE THIS BEFORE?
SWITCH
ON/OFF
SOMEWHERE NEARBY . . .
YOU'RE NOT GETTING AWAY THAT EASILY.
I'LL TURN HIM INTO CAT SOUP!
NOT IF I GET HIM FIRST.
HUFF-HUFF I SAID I WAS SORRY.
AHA! I'LL LOSE THEM IN THE MAIN SQUARE.

WHOA!
HOLD IT STEADY.
OH MY GOSH! I WANT MY MOMMY!
SHUT IT OFF, MISSY!
5
AHA!
BEEP!
I TURNED IT OFF!
GIZMO?! OH NO!
RUMBLE
STOP!
YIKES!!
CRASH!

LATER, AFTER EVERYTHING SETTLED DOWN . . .
MEDIC

LOOK AT THIS DISASTER, IVAN!
HOW DID THIS HAPPEN?!
I . . . UUHHH . . .
BEEP! BOOP!
OH MY!
YOU MUST SEE THIS.
A SECURITY VIDEO?

THE EVIDENCE!
BREAKING AND ENTERING?
INTERIOR CAMERA 2
INTERIOR CAMERA 18
AND LOOK, IT'S THE CAT!
IN ALL MY YEARS, I HAVE NEVER SEEN SUCH A RECKLESS ACT!
YOU DELINQUENTS ARE THE CAUSE OF ALL THIS!

NOT TO MENTION MY ALLERGIES!
ACHOO!
YOU'RE NO HERO.
YOU'RE JUST A MISCHIEVOUS LITTLE GIRL.
WAIT, IT WASN'T MISSY'S IDEA . . .
HUSH IT, MELVIRA.
I KNOW YOU'RE UP TO SOMETHING. I DON'T KNOW WHAT, BUT I DON'T LIKE IT.
YOU'RE ALL KICKED OUT OF CAMP.
YOU'LL NEVER BE SUPERHEROES!

CHAPTER 7
THE SUPERHERO BLUES
BACK IN ~~IDLEVILLE~~ GLUMVILLE, MISSY HAS NOT BEEN HER USUAL SELF.
HOW IS SHE DOING?
SHE HASN'T SAID A WORD.
THEY DON'T DO SCIENCE CAMP LIKE THEY USED TO.
YEAH.

HEY, LOOK AT ME.
I'M ANNOYING!
ME
HUG
LOOK!
I'M PUNCHING YOUR FAVORITE TEDDY BEAR!
SAVE ME FROM YOUR RAD BRO. AHHH!
SIGH
HUG ME
LOOK! I'M DOING A BUTT DANCE!
MOM!
I THINK MISSY IS BROKEN!
EVEN RAFI'S CONSTANT TEASING ISN'T WORKING.
THIS IS WORSE THAN I THOUGHT.

BACK IN THEIR UNDERGROUND LAIR . . .
HEY MISSY, WANT SOME PURPLE YAM ICE CREAM?
NO.
DAY 4
WHAT ABOUT POPCORN AND CHOCOLATE RAISINS?
NO!
DAY 8
SLICED MANGO AND SHRIMP ANCHOVY DIP?
NO!
DAY 12
MISSY, YOU'VE BEEN IN PAJAMAS FOR TWO WEEKS.
AND YOU HAVEN'T LEFT THAT SPOT FOR DAYS . . .
AND YOU SMELL KINDA . . .
EWW.

OF COURSE I HAVEN'T MOVED.
THAT'S WHAT YOU DO WHEN YOU'RE DEPRESSED!
DEPRESSED?
BUT WE HAVE OUR OWN UNDERGROUND LAB NOW!
WE CAN HAVE FUN. BE AS LOUD AS WE WANT.
BUILD STUFF. DO CRAZY EXPERIMENTS.
PLAY GAMES AND EAT TONS OF SNACKS!

DUDE! DID YOU FORGET THE LAST CHAPTER?
DECEPTION.
ROBOT BATTLE.
GETTING KICKED OUT!
IT'S SO EMBARRASSING.
EXACTLY.
BUT THAT'S ALL SO BACK STORY-ISH.
BUT I JUST WANTED TO BE SUPER!
MAYBE IF YOU FOCUSED ON SOMETHING ELSE.
YOU MIGHT EVEN FIND SOMETHING YOU'D LIKE,
WHAT DO YOU SAY?
SIGH
YOU'RE RIGHT.
I'M NOT GONNA LET THIS GET TO ME.
NOW YOU'RE TALKING.

MISSY'S "DON'T GET BUMMED OUT" TO-DO LIST:
#1 STAND-UP COMEDIAN
SO I TOLD THAT OLD LADY, "THAT'S ONE SCARY MOLE!"
HA-HA-HA
I LOVE THAT JOKE!
#2 YOUTUBER
. . . WE'RE GOING TO UNBOX THIS NEW GADGET FROM FLEABAY!
BUT FIRST, MAKE SURE TO CLICK SUBSCRIBE!
#3 POKER PLAYER
YOU HAVEN'T BLINKED FOR TWO HOURS.
BLINKING IS A DEAD GIVEAWAY.
#4 HAIRDRESSER
IS THAT CURLY ENOUGH?

#5 ARTIST
A MASTERPIECE! I WILL SELL IT FOR A MILLION DOLLARS!
#6 DOG WALKER
WHOA! SLOW DOWN, GUYS!
SPLASH!
AGH!
IS THIS MY LIFE NOW?
MISSY?!
LONG TIME NO SEE!
MELVIRA?!
YOU HAVEN'T ANSWERED MY CALLS, EMAILS, TEXT MESSAGES, CARRIER PIGEONS, MESSAGES IN A BOTTLE . . .
SORRY. I'M STILL IN A FUNK ABOUT WHAT HAPPENED.

MISSY, YOU'RE VERY TALENTED.
DON'T LET WHAT HAPPENED AT CAMP GET YOU DOWN.
BESIDES, I THINK YOU CAN **STILL** BE SUPER. . . .
I CAN'T. I GOT KICKED OUT, REMEMBER?
YOU'RE LOOKING AT THIS ALL WRONG.
YOU HAVE TO UNLEASH YOURSELF. BE SUPER IN YOUR OWN WAY. . . . **A SUPERVILLAIN!**
ISN'T THAT BAD?
PSHAW!
IT JUST MEANS YOU CAN BE SUPER **WITHOUT ANY OF THE RULES.**
RIP
RULES

YOU GET TO BE THE BOSS.
NO NEED FOR A HERO CERTIFICATE.
NO BOOT CAMP.
NONE OF THAT JUNK!
I LIKE THAT. MY OWN PATH, MY OWN DESTINY.
REMEMBER WHEN WE BATTLED THE ROBOT
AND WON?
YEAH, IT WAS AWESOME!
WE CAN DO THAT AGAIN, TIMES A THOUSAND!
WHAT DO YOU SAY, MISSY? ARE YOU IN?
I'M IN!
SISTERS IN TROUBLE!

THE VILLAIN STARTER PACK!

TO BE A SERIOUS VILLAIN, YOU NEED A SERIOUS OUTFIT. GOOD THING I'M THE **MASTER OF DISGUISE.** LET'S TRY A FEW . . .

EVIL SCIENTIST OUTFIT WITH CRAZY HAIRDO

EVIL WRENCH OUTFIT

BALD GUY OUTFIT

BEACH OUTFIT

EVIL CLOWN OUTFIT

CHICKEN OUTFIT

EVERY VILLAIN NEEDS A PATENTED LAUGH.
MUA-HA-HA!
HO-HO-HO-HO
MEOW MEOW
KE-KE KE-KE KE-KE
SUPERVILLAIN MASTER PLAN
BY OUR NATURE, VILLAINS ARE VISIONARIES!
WE MAKE COMPLEX PLANS AND HAVE GRAND IDEAS!
HEROES USE POWERS, BUT WE RELY ON OUR SMARTS.
IT'S ALL ABOUT PLANNING AND PREPARATION!
MISSY CAN DO THE THINKIN'.
I'LL DO THE SLEEPIN'.
AND WHAT SEPARATES A REGULAR VILLAIN FROM A SUPERVILLAIN?
STYLE!

THIS IS IT . . . OUR FIRST MISSION.
I'M PUMPED!
DID YOU THINK OF A VILLAIN NAME?
NOT YET, THAT'S WAY TOO MUCH COMMITMENT.
IT'S OKAY. IT'LL COME TO YOU.
YOUR FIRST MISSION IS HOW YOU WILL BE DEFINED AS A SUPERVILLAIN FOREVER.
MAKE IT GOOD.
RIGHT. FIRST IMPRESSIONS LAST.
OH YEAH!
BUT DO WE REALLY HAVE TO JUMP FROM A ROOFTOP?
IT'S CALLED MAKING AN ENTRANCE.
SHOVE
WHOA!!
MELVIRAAA!!!

CHAPTER 8

HERO NO MORE!

STYLISH LANDING!
AREN'T WE SUPPOSED TO LAND INSIDE A BANK?
CHANGE OF PLANS. WE'RE DOING SOMETHING MORE SINISTER AND EVILER!
HA-HA-HA!
AND SO MISSY AND GIZMO ENTERED ONE STORE . . .
ZEN SPA AND TANNING
AFTER THE OTHER . . .
SHE SELLS SHOES & SANDALS
AND DID THE MOST UNTHINKABLE THING YOU CAN THINK OF!
NO! YOU'RE NOT GOING TO . . .
YES! YES! YES! HA-HA-HA!
SANDAL
SHOE

THE NEXT DAY . . .
NEWS 9
ON LOCATION: WORLD-FAMOUS DOWNTOWN SHOPPING CENTER
WORLD-FAMOUS DOWNTOWN SHOPPING CENTER
THIS IS FOX BLISTER REPORTING.
LAST NIGHT SOMEONE DID THE **MOST VILLAINOUS ACTS!** LET'S TAKE A LOOK . . .
OUR TANNING MACHINES WERE TAMPERED WITH.
GREEN? I LOOK HIDEOUS!
UNBELIEVABLE! **BLUE** IS SO LAST YEAR.
WE'RE RUINED!
ALL THAT IS LEFT ARE **RIGHT-FOOT SHOES!**
SNEAKERS
GOOD GRIEF! SOMEONE REPLACED OUR PASTA WITH GLUTEN-FREE! **GLUTEN-FREEEEE! WHO WOULD DO SUCH A THING?!**
IT TASTES LIKE CARDBOARD.

WHO ARE THESE CRIMINAL MASTERMINDS?
THE ONLY CLUE IS THIS HALF-EATEN RICE BALL WITH CAT HAIR.
THE CITY WILL NEVER SLEEP UNTIL THE PERPETRATORS OF SUCH MISCHIEF AND MAYHEM ARE FOUND!
OH YEAH, OH YEAH! WE DID IT! WE DID IT!
I LOVE THAT NAME— MISCHIEF AND MAYHEM!
SHOES? TANNING? PASTA? YOU WERE SUPPOSED TO ROB THE BANK!
BAWK!
THIS IS MORE FUN.
WE NEED TO THINK BIG . . .
FLEX OUR MUSCLES. SHOW THE WORLD THAT WE'RE THE BIGGEST, BADDEST VILLAINS AROUND.
I LIKE YOU, KID. YOU HAVE GUMPTION.
WE'RE GOING PLACES AS LONG AS YOU FOLLOW MY LEAD.
OK, CAN YOU LET ME CHEW?

SOON, MISSY AND GIZMO BEGIN TO TAKE ON MORE ELABORATE MISSIONS.
THIS WAY! GET 'EM!
IT WAS A CAT BURGLAR! I SAW IT.
ROOF EXIT
STOP!
THIS IS STRESS LEVEL 100, DUDE.
YOU'RE SUPPOSED TO DISTRACT THEM.
SORRY, I WAS DISTRACTED BY THE COTTON CANDY MACHINE!
DIAMOND FACTORY
STRESS LEVEL 1000!
GLIDERS ARE NOT ENGAGING.
SWOOP!
BAWK!
I'M GLAD OUR AVIAN FRIEND SHOWED UP.

CITY HALL
FOX REPORTING. I AM WITH MAYOR POPSICLE.
THESE RECENT ACTIVITIES FROM MISCHIEF AND MAYHEM ARE TRULY DISTURBING.
INDEED. DISTURBING.
LAST WEEK THEY STOLE THE SEMI-AMAZING COMPUTER CHIP AND LAST NIGHT THEY STOLE THE VALUABLE TURTLE-PURPLE DIAMOND!
VERY VALUABLE.
AND THEY EVEN VANDALIZED MY CAR! LOOK!
MISCHIEF WAS HERE
AND YOUR BACK!
THE MAYOR STINKS
OH.

WELL, AREN'T YOU GONNA DO ANYTHING?
YOU'RE THE MAYOR!
WELL, I DID EMAIL THE LEAGUE OF HEROES SO THEY CAN STOP THE BAD GUYS.
I HOPE IT DIDN'T GO INTO THEIR SPAM FOLDER.
EMAIL
SENT→
DON'T YOU HAVE A SECRET RED PHONE YOU CAN USE TO CALL THEM?
THIS IS AN EMERGENCY.
ERHM . . .
NO.
THERE YOU HAVE IT, FOLKS. WITH THE LEAGUE OF HEROES SOON ON OUR SIDE . . .
THE DAYS OF MISCHIEF AND MAYHEM ARE NUMBERED!

BATTERY INDUSTRY
BOOM!
FASTER, MISCHIEF!
IT'S THE FASTEST IT'LL GO!
ZOOM
WHOA!
FLIP
THE BATTERY?
SAFE AS A BABY!
RETURN EL GRANDE BATTERY!
CATHODES, ANODES, ATTACK!

AHHH! THESE LITTLE BUGGERS ARE ZAPPING ME.
KZZZZT
I'M SHOCKED!
WHACK!
CHOK!
ZZZTT
GIVE UP, YOU LOW-ENERGY VILLAINS!
HEY, DOC, WHAT HAPPENS WHEN YOU CROSS THE BLUE WIRE WITH THE RED WIRE?
TELL HIM, MISCHIEF.

NO!! THAT'S DANGEROUS.
DO IT, MISCHIEF! TOAST THAT DUDE.
BZZZTTT!
KA-BOOM!
AND THAT'S HOW WE ROLL.
THEY'LL WAKE UP WITH BAD HEAD-ACHES.

WITH EVERY SINISTER CAPER, MISCHIEF AND MAYHEM BECAME EVEN MORE INFAMOUS!
STAR
NEWS
DAILY NEWS
MISCHIEF & MAYHEM AT IT AGAIN!
CAT GOSSIP
WHO IS MAYHEM?
IDLEVILLE JOURNAL
VILLAINY MONTHLY
50 WAYS TO
WE'RE SUPERPOPULAR! LOOK AT ALL THIS FAN MAIL!
MAIL
WHOA! A MISCHIEF LOVE LETTER!
GIMME THAT.
YOINK!
HEY!
DEAR MISCHIEF, YOU'RE SO CUTE AND STYLISH. WILL YOU MARRY ME? PLEASE SAY YES. WRITE BACK SOON. YOUR BELOVED, GOOSE. P.S. YOU NEED A NEW SIDE-CAT.
EW!
HEY, I KNOW HOW WE CAN SKYROCKET OUR POPULARITY TO LEVEL 9000!
OH YEAH?

LEVEL 9000 MASTER PLAN
TA-DA!
THIS IS GOOD! BUT WILL MELVIRA BE OKAY WITH IT?
SHE'S NOT OUR BOSS.
BESIDES, WE'VE DONE LOTS OF STUFF FOR HER.
YEAH . . . WE GOT ALL THOSE THINGS—
THE BATTERY, COMPUTER CHIP, EVEN THE DIAMOND!
BORROWED PARTS:
BATTERY
CHIP
COMPLETE ASSEMBLY: ???
I WONDER WHAT SHE'S UP TO?
IT DOES SEEM WEIRD.
BUT HEY, IT'S MELVIRA . . . WE'RE ON THE SAME TEAM.
AND WE CAN ASK HER ABOUT IT LATER.
BUT FOR NOW, IT'S TIME FOR OUR OWN LITTLE HEIST!
OH YEAH!

BIG TP FACTORY
THE GREAT PAPER CAPER!
SECURITY
ZZZ
STOP!
CLINK
CLINK
CLINK
SLIDE!
HERE WE ARE. THE TOILET PAPER FACTORY!

GENIUS.
NO ONE WOULD THINK OF STEALING THE CITY'S SUPPLY OF TOILET PAPER!
SHE WHO CONTROLS THE TP, CONTROLS THE WORLD!
TIME TO USE THE TP SHRINK AND SNAG RAY!
AMAZING!
ZAP!
THIS WAS THE EASIEST HEIST EVER!
AND WE'RE STOCKED UP WITH TP TO LAST THE NEXT 10 YEARS.

BUT AS THEY ESCAPE . . .
THE HEROES HAVE ARRIVED. I AM STRONG DUDE.
DUDE
SHA-SHA! PREPARE TO MEET CHILLAXE.
I AM FISH!
BOOYA! FIREBALL KID IN THE HOUSE.
ZOOOM
DRUM ROLL . . . SPEED PASS IS HERE.
MISCHIEF VS THE LEAGUE OF HEROES!
WHOA.
WHAT'S UP, GUYS?
ARE YOU HERE TO JOIN THE PARTY?
NO PARTY . . .
JUST BATTLE!

OUR FIRST BATTLE WITH THE INFAMOUS MISCHIEF AND MAYHEM!
DUDE
SMASH!
I'LL GET YOU MY AUTO-GRAPHED PHOTO LATER!
TASTE MY KNUCKLE SANDWICH, TONKATSU STYLE!
PONK!
DUDE
SHOOM!
STOP MOVING! I'M TRYING TO BARBECUE YOU.
CHECK IT OUT. SHAVED-ICE BLAST!
THIS GOES WELL WITH RED BEANS AND MILK.
FIZZZZ
I GOT HIM!
NO, I DON'T.
BOINK!
WHAT AN ICY PERSONALITY!
OOPS!

HI-YAH!
OOOOFF!
OWWWIE!
TAKE THIS, MEGAMESH!
TRIP!
WHOA! WHY ME?
CRASH!
WATCH OUT!
HA! DO YA GIVE UP, DO-GOODERS?
YOU KNOW, THAT PARTY INVITE IS STILL OPEN.
YEAH, I'M DOWN FOR A TIME OUT!
SOUNDS GOOD TO ME.

SO THEY DECIDED IT WAS A GOOD IDEA TO BREAK FOR MILK AND COOKIES.
THESE ARE FRESH. CHOMP
JUST LIKE MY MOM USED TO MAKE. THIS CALMS ME DOWN. THANKS.
DUD
I'LL TELL YOU THE SECRET— LOTS OF BUTTER!
CHOMP
OUR VILLAIN BATTLES ARE NEVER THIS TASTY.
FANCY OUTFITS BY THE WAY.
THANKS. MELVIRA HELPED US MAKE THEM.
YOU KNOW, WE ALL FELT BAD ABOUT THE WHOLE INCIDENT AT BOOT CAMP.
AND YOU SAVED US FROM THE ROBOT.

I HOPE EVERYTHING WENT BACK TO NORMAL AFTER ALL THAT CRAZINESS.
OH, YOU DIDN'T HEAR?
AFTER GRADUATION, PEOPLE FROM THE COUNCIL OF HEROES APPEARED.
THEY DECIDED TO SHUT DOWN BOOT CAMP, INDEFINITELY!
SUPERHERO BOOT CAMP
CLOSED
NO ENTRY
THEN STUFF WENT MISSING— TOOLS AND GADGETS . . .
BAWK!
SHHHH . . .
EVEN THAT ROBOT GUARD DISAPPEARED. . . .

I THINK GRU AND IVAN ARE NOW VOLUNTEERING AT THE SHELTER.
SO SAD.
HOW THINGS HAVE CHANGED.
UH-HUH. CHOMP
WHAT A **BEAUTIFUL** NIGHT.
YUP.
DUDE
WELL, IT'S BEEN FUN. BYE, HEROES!
GLAD TO SEE YA, WOULDN'T WANNA BE YA!
SHOULD WE BE **CHASING** THEM?
NAH. WE CAN DO IT TOMORROW.

CHAPTER 9

MELVIRA'S SECRET PLAN REVEALED!

HEROES CAN'T STOP MISCHIEF AND MAYHEM
Idle Times
MAYOR IN A STICKY TP SITUATION
BATHROOMS BURGLED BY BADDIES
I'VE BEEN USING BANANA PEELS IN PLACE OF TP.
I DON'T KNOW WHAT ELSE TO DO!
9
NEWS
HELP!! OUT OF TP!!
HA! I TOLD 'EM, BUT NO ONE EVER LISTENS.
NO ONE!
GOOD THING I SAVED A LOT OF TP.
THE END IS HERE!
9
CALL THE MAYOR, CALL THE PRESIDENT. THIS IS A NATIONAL EMERGENCY.
9

YOU REALLY OUTDID YOURSELVES. LIVING UP TO YOUR NAMES,
MISCHIEF AND MAYHEM.
WE COULDN'T HAVE DONE IT WITHOUT YOUR HELP. YOU WERE THERE FOR ME WHEN I WAS DOWN IN THE DUMPS.
HA! YOU SAID DUMPS.
I HAVE A SURPRISE FOR YOU.
CHECK THIS OUT.
BZZT. BZZZT.

IT'S OUR OLD FRIEND.
IT'S THE CAMP ROBOT!
SO SPOOKY.
ROBOT WAS ABANDONED
BY THE **HEROES.**
JUST LIKE YOU AND ME.
I TOOK HIM IN AND MADE SOME UPGRADES.
US "REJECTS" HAVE TO STICK TOGETHER.

WHAT YOU DO IS FUN . . .
BUT YOU NEED TO FOCUS ON THE BIGGER PICTURE.
BAD
BAWK!
AND WHAT'S THIS?
MILK AND COOKIES?!
THAT'S KIDDIE STUFF.
DUD
WELL, THEY ARE OLD FRIENDS. . . .
M
NO!
HEROES ARE NOT FRIENDS!

I THINK SHE'S GOING **CRAZY.**
SHHHH.
WE'RE **SUPERVILLAINS** NOW.
WE CAN'T BE HANGING OUT WITH HEROES.
DON'T FORGET HOW THEY TREATED US. THEY THINK THEY'RE SPECIAL . . .
WITH THEIR "POWERS."
ULTIMATE WEAPON
CHIP
BUT THANKS TO YOU . . . WE CAN MAKE THEM UNSPECIAL.
WE NOW HAVE ALL THE PARTS TO COMPLETE **THE ULTIMATE WEAPON!**

WE JUST GOTTA PUT IT TOGETHER.
BAWK!
WOW! AMAZING REVEAL.
I HONESTLY DID NOT SEE THAT COMING.
NO HEROES
OUR MISSION IS TO RID THE WORLD OF EVERYTHING SUPER!
AND THE PERFECT PLACE TO UNLEASH OUR WEAPON IS . . .
THE ANNUAL SUPER FESTIVAL!
THE ANNUAL SUPER FESTIVAL
CELEBRATE EVERYTHING SUPER.
FAMILY FRIENDLY. EVEN FOR PETS.
SPECIAL SUPERHERO GUESTS FROM
THE LEAGUE OF HEROES
SPECIAL APPEARANCE BY MAYOR POPSICLE!
RIDES, CARNIVAL GAMES, COTTON CANDY

I DON'T KNOW ABOUT THIS. IT SEEMS EXTREME.
WE'RE ALL FOR FUN AND GAMES BUT . . .
NO MORE GOOFING AROUND! NO MORE MISCHIEF AND MAYHEM . . .
ONLY DESTRUCTION AND CHAOS!
MELVIRA . . . I CAN'T.
THIS IS TOO MUCH.
BAWK!
YOU'RE UPSETTING CLAW.
WE DON'T WANT TO HURT ANYONE OR DESTROY STUFF . . . AT LEAST NOT ON PURPOSE.
CAN YOU IMAGINE THE INSURANCE CLAIMS?

IT'S ALL FOR A BETTER WORLD . . . WHERE PEOPLE LIKE US WON'T BE HIDING IN THE SHADOWS OF HEROES.
I'M SORRY . . . I CAN'T BE PART OF THIS.
WEAK SAUCE!
DON'T FIZZ OUT ON ME NOW.
YOU KNOW, IF IT WASN'T FOR ME, YOU'D BE NOTHING.
I MADE YOU, AND I CAN UNMAKE YOU.
MELVIRA, THIS IS WAY TOO WILD!
I THINK WE SHOULD GO.
UGH. YOU FORCED MY HAND.
ROBOT, DO SOMETHING HORRIBLE!

MISCHIEF VS ROBOT AGAIN!
DESTROY!
BESERK MODE ENGAGED!
AH!
CRASH!
ARE YOU NUTS?
SHWACK!
OOFFF!
BAWK!
SCRATCH!!
FLYING KICK!
AAAAHHHH!!
AS YOU CAN SEE, ROBOT IS FASTER THAN EVER!

CLANK!
SPINNER ATTACK, ENGAGE!
GRABBY ARMS, ENGAGE!
SMASH!
AH!
HA, GOTCHA!
GRAB
GRAB
UGH!
WOMP!
PULL
WHOA!

HEY, ROBOT! NO HEADBUTTS,
THAT'S CHEATING!
OW!
THE OFF SWITCH IS GONE!
SCRATCH
SCRATCH
SCRATCH
FWISH!!
BZZZZT.
BLASTER!
WE'RE CORNERED!

KA-CHOOM!
KA-CHOOM!
UHN
GIVE IT UP.
YOU'RE NO MATCH.
FIRST, I HAVE TO TELL YOU SOMETHING.
MISCHIEF'S FAMOUS FINAL WORDS?
STICKY SLUDGE!
I'VE BEEN PRACTICING MY AIM.
AHHH! DISGUSTING.
SPLAT!
SPLAT!
BAWK!

I'M STUCK!
ROBOT, STOP HER!
SPLAT!
SPLAT!
VISION IMPAIRED!
ROBOT STUCK!
CRASH!

UH-OH, NO MORE STICKY SLUDGE.
TIME TO GO.
I GOT YOU, BUDDY.
GET BACK HERE!
I'LL GET YOU, MISCHIEF!!!!
MISCHIEF!

CHAPTER 10

WHO WILL SAVE US?

LATER THAT NIGHT, MISSY RETURNS TO HER SECRET LAIR . . .

I GUESS WHEN YOU MAKE FRIENDS WITH SUPERVILLAINS . . .
THEY **BREAK YOUR HEART** AND WRECK YOUR SECRET LAIR.
GRRR
I CAN'T BELIEVE SHE TOOK ALL OUR GEAR!!
MY GAMESTATION 4 IS GONE, MY COMIC BOOK COLLECTION IS MISSING.
AH! EVEN MY SCRATCHING POST WAS TAKEN.
TIME TO RETIRE OUR VILLAIN ALTER EGOS.
AND ALL WE GOT IS A LIFETIME'S WORTH OF TP. . . .

OH NO!
OH NO!
WHAT'S WRONG?!
WHEW!
SHE LEFT THE PICKLED BLACK EGGS ALONE. THANK GOODNESS.
WHAT ARE WE GOING TO DO?
I'M NOT SURE.
SHE TOOK MOST OF OUR GADGETS, **THERE'S NO WAY WE CAN STOP HER.**
YEAH, AND AFTER EVERYTHING WE'VE BEEN THROUGH . . . I FEEL **TRULY SCARED.**

DAYS PASSED....
MELVIRA SEEMED TO HAVE DISAPPEARED.
FOR THE FIRST TIME, THEY WERE NOT THINKING OF MISCHIEF OR MAYHEM.

BUT BACK IN THE WORLD OF HEROES AND VILLAINS . . .
SURRENDER, CRIMINAL.
GAH! WE'RE TRAPPED.
WHAT NOW?
GIVE UP, CRIMINAL.
THERE IS NO ESCAPE FROM FLYING DAN.
ACTUALLY, YOU'RE EXACTLY WHERE WE WANT.
ZOOP ZIP ZWOOSH!
TRANSFORM!
TA-DA!!
HUH? WHAT'S GOING ON?

ZAP!
SAY CHEESE!
AAAIIEEE!!
CRASH!
TRASH
WE DID IT.
THE ZAPPER WORKED!
BAWK!
HELP! THEY STOLE MY POWER!

SOMEWHERE ELSE . . .
HA-HA! FEAR NOT.
HEFTY HAL IS HERE!
HOORAY!
ZOOP
ZIP
ZWOOSH!
OH, HE'S SOOO GOOD. "HE SAVED US."
YUCK!
BUT CAN HE SAVE HIMSELF?

ZAP!
UH-OH!
CRASH
OUCH!
HEFTY HAL DOESN'T FEEL SO GOOD.
NEWS 9
WHY ARE HEROES LOSING THEIR POWERS?
FOX REPORTING WITH BREAKING NEWS!
SUPERHEROES FROM ALL OVER HAVE BEEN LOSING THEIR POWERS!
9

LIKE, I WAS TOTALLY BREATHING UNDERWATER, THEN ALL OF A SUDDEN I COULDN'T ANYMORE!
AND I WAS LIKE, WHOA, UNCOOL, DUDE.
NEWS 9
INTERVIEW WITH HERO H_2O
ONE SECOND, I WAS INVISIBLE,
AND NOW EVERYONE CAN SEE ME!
DO YOU KNOW YOU'RE NAKED?
NEWS 9
INTERVIEW WITH HERO INVISIBLE MAN
CENSORED!
I'M NOT EVEN A SUPERHERO AND I'M MAD!
THERE YOU HAVE IT, FOLKS.
SUPER-HEROES WITHOUT SUPER-POWERS?
WHO WILL SAVE US NOW?
NEWS 9
INTERVIEW WITH RANDOM PERSON

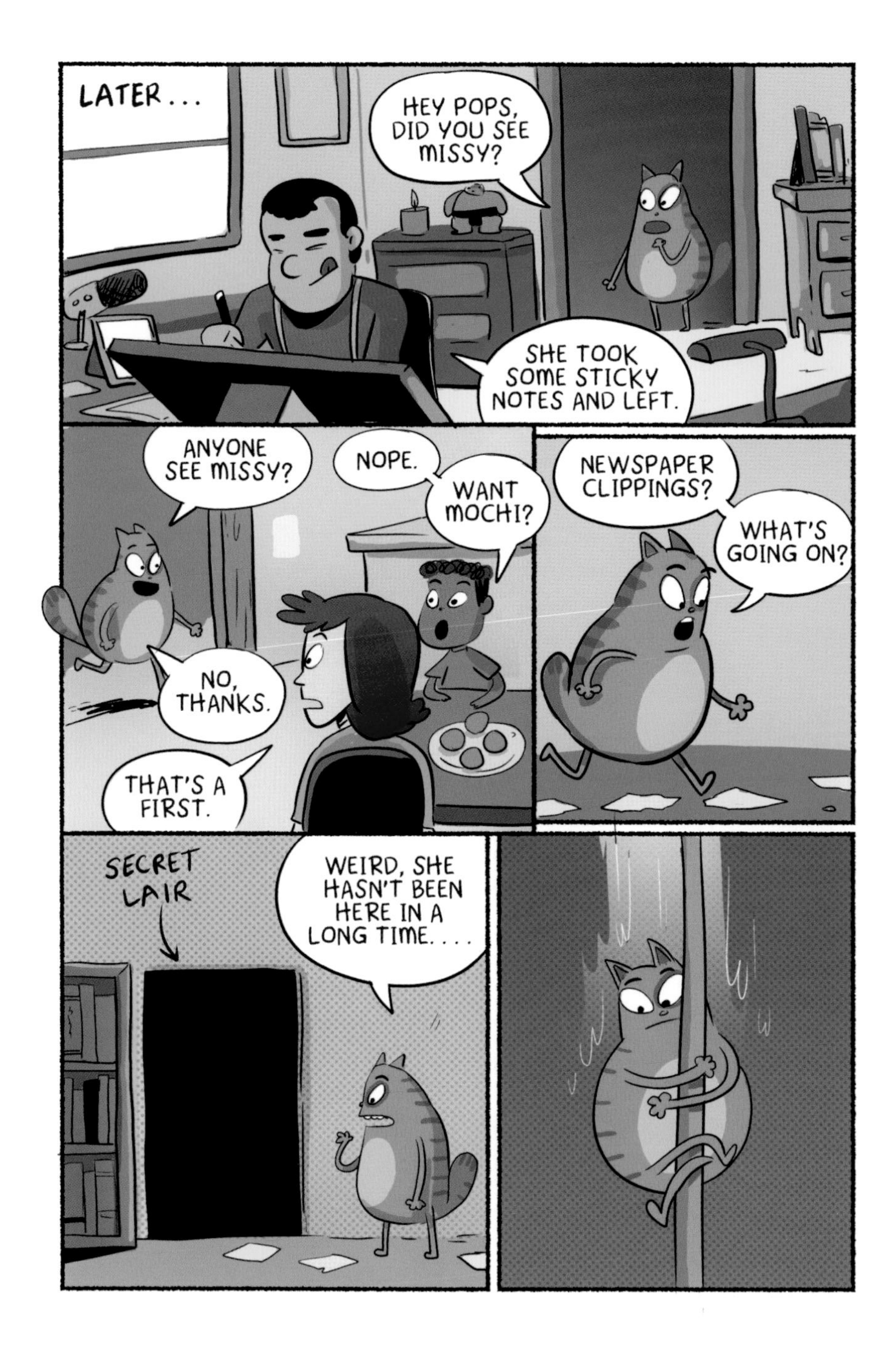
LATER...
HEY POPS, DID YOU SEE MISSY?
SHE TOOK SOME STICKY NOTES AND LEFT.
ANYONE SEE MISSY?
NOPE.
WANT MOCHI?
NO, THANKS.
THAT'S A FIRST.
NEWSPAPER CLIPPINGS?
WHAT'S GOING ON?
SECRET LAIR
WEIRD, SHE HASN'T BEEN HERE IN A LONG TIME. . . .

HEROES LIST
TP SHOOTER 3000 PLANS:
WHAT'S THIS?
ARE YOU BUILDING A NEW GADGET?
SOMETHING'S BEEN BUGGIN' ME.
I DID SOME DIGGING . . .
TRACKED ALL THE HEROES WHO LOST THEIR POWERS.
AND LOOK! THEY'RE ALL IN THE SAME AREA AS THE TREEHOUSE OF DOOM!
MELVIRA'S LAIR

CLICK
THANKS FOR TUNING IN. . . .
IT'S A WONDERFUL DAY AND WE ARE LIVE FROM THE ANNUAL SUPER FESTIVAL.
SUPER FESTIVAL
LIVE
WELL, I'M OUT. THIS IS BORING. . . .
STAY. WE HAVE TO MAKE SURE.
FINE.
THIS IS FOX WORKING OVERTIME!
LET'S TAKE A CLOSER LOOK.
SUPER FESTIVAL
LIVE

HOTDOGS
TOYS
SUPER
FESTIVAL
YOU CAN SEE WE HAVE LOTS OF THINGS GOING ON TODAY.
WE HAVE THE WORLD-FAMOUS SUPER FLASH DANCE GROUP.
KIDS ENJOYING SOME TIME IN THE SUPER PETTING ZOO . . .
THE OLD PEOPLE DRINKING SUPERFANCY DRINKS . . .

TEENAGERS PLAYING SUPERFUN CARNIVAL GAMES.
VOLCANO
WE EVEN HAVE SUPERYUMMY STREET FOOD!
WHATCHA GOT THERE?
SUPER ORANGE CHICKEN AND TRIPLE CORN DOGS!
9
LIVE STREAM
AS YOU CAN SEE, EVERYTHING IS **SUPER** AT THE SUPER FESTIVAL!
LOOK. IT'S MAYOR POPSICLE.
HE'S ABOUT TO GIVE A COMMENDATION TO THE LEAGUE OF HEROES.
ANNUAL SUPER FESTIVAL!!!
LET'S GET A CLOSER PEEK.
9

TO HONOR THEIR AWESOME HERO STUFF, I AWARD THE *KEY TO THE CITY* TO **THE LEAGUE OF HEROES!**
HOORAY!
OH YEAH.
ALL RIGHT!
RAD.
I WASN'T SURE IF WE'D GET IT.
DUDE
BUBBLES!
SEE?! THE SUPERHEROES GOT IT ALL **UNDER CONTROL.**
THERE'S NOTHING TO WORRY ABOUT.
I GUESS YOU'RE RIGHT.

WAIT!
IT LOOKS LIKE SOMEONE JUST SHOWED UP ONSTAGE!
IS THIS A NEW SUPERHERO?
BADUM
BADUM
BADUM
WHO IS THIS?
IS IT A NEW VILLAIN?
SHE'S UP TO NO GOOD.
I AM MELVIRA, THE WORLD'S NUMBER ONE SUPERVILLAIN!
AND I AM HERE TO STOP THIS CHARADE!

CHAPTER 11
RUMBLE, RUMBLE! LOTSA TROUBLE
MELVIRA?
WHAT IS SHE UP TO?
DUDE
HAVEN'T YOU HEARD?
I'VE BEEN ZAPPING SUPERHEROES INTO SUPER ZEROES.
SOON, EVERYTHING SUPER WILL BE GONE.
LET ME SHOW YOU.
ZAP!
GASP!
MY SUPER STREET FOOD VANISHED!
AS MAYOR, I ORDER YOU TO STOP!

YOU CAN'T STOP ME. I AM FABULOUSLY EVIL!!
BAWK!
MELVIRA VS THE LEAGUE OF HEROES
YOU'LL HAVE TO GET PAST US FIRST.
DUDE
YOU DON'T SCARE US.
WE ARE THE BEST, SOMETIMES.
HEROES, CHARGE!
ROBOT, SHOW THEM WHAT YOU CAN DO.

CLUNK!
CLUNK!
ROBOT BABIES?!
OH, THEY'RE SOOO CUTE.
THEY'RE NOT SCARY AT ALL.
CAN I BRING THEM HOME?
MINIBOTS, GET 'EM!

HEY, STOP!
AAHH!
GET AWAY!
SORRY, LITTLE DUDE.
ARREEEH!
DUDE
BONK!
NO MORE GAMES.
PONG!
FWACK!
PING!
LET'S HEAT THINGS UP.
FWOOOSH!!!

THWAM!!
THAT ROBOT NEEDS A PERSONALITY CHECK.
IT HAS A BAD TEMPER.
MAYBE I CAN HELP. . . .
TIME TO CHILLAXE!
ICE BLAST!
BAM!
FIREBALL!
CHOOM!
CHOOM!!

AHHH!!! MY BEAUTIFUL HAIR!
SUPER-SPEED!
HI-YAH! BIG PUNCH!
EW!
HANDS OFF THE FACE!
OOPS!
DODGE
DUDE
TWAP!!
KRA-KOOM!!
SOMEONE DO SOMETHING!

I GOT THIS. I SUMMON
SUPER MEGAWHALE!
FESTIVAL
SLAM!!
CALLING A MEGAWHALE IS NEVER OKAY!
SHOULD I GET SHARK?
NO!

WE HAVE TO HELP!
LOOK, THE HEROES HAVE THIS COVERED.
YOU KNOW MELVIRA'S GOT SOMETHING UP HER SNEAKY SLEEVES.
I LEFT THAT SUPERVILLAIN LIFE A LONG TIME AGO. . . .
GIZMO, IT WAS LAST WEEK. I NEED YA BUDDY, BUT IT'S YOUR CHOICE.
WE SHOULDN'T GO. MELVIRA TOOK ALL OUR STUFF. WE HAVE NO GADGETS LEFT TO STOP HER.
THERE'S ONE THING SHE CAN'T TAKE AWAY . . . **BRAIN POWER.**
MISCHIEF WILL FIGURE THIS OUT.

FOX REPORTING! WHILE OUR HEROES ARE BUSY FIGHTING, MELVIRA IS UP TO SOMETHING EVEN MORE SINISTER.
SUPER MARKET
ZAP
I HATE SUPERMARKETS!
HA!
MINI - MART
MEGAMALL SUPERCENTER
ZAP
THIS IS FUN!
STRIP MALL

DUCK FACE!
SNAP!
EVERYONE LOVES US.
BLECH!
I HATE SUPERFICIAL PEOPLE!
ZAP
?
SUPERHIGHWAY 15
ZAP!
WHERE'D ALL THE ROADS GO?
MUA-HA-HA-HA! AND NOW FOR THE MAIN EVENT.

ALL THIS FIGHTING GOT ME HUNGRY.
THE BARBECUED RIBS HERE ARE ZESTY.
WE'LL GET BARBECUED IF WE DON'T STOP THE ROBOT.
DUDE
SO, ANY IDEAS?
HEY!! I HAVE AN IDEA.
TAKE THIS!!!
ZAP!!!

MY POWER WENT KAPUT.
MINE TOO.
WHAT ARE WE GONNA DO?
THIS IS NOT GOOD.
WE STILL HAVE WHALE!
DUDE
ZAP!
OH NO!
BREAKING NEWS! OUR HEROES HAVE BEEN DEFEATED AND CAPTURED BY MELVIRA!
9

BAWK!
SNAP!
SNAP
SNAP
ACM
FOX, STOP TALKING AND CALL FOR HELP!
I CAN'T BELIEVE WE FAILED!
MELVIRA CHEATED! SHE'S A POWER THIEF!
I'M A VILLAIN, I'M SUPPOSED TO CHEAT.
CLAW, FEED THEM TO THE CROCS!
KA-CLUNK!
BRRRRR

DUDE, SO UNEXPECTED.
WHERE DID THESE CROCS COME FROM?
GOT 'EM FROM CROCS-R-US.
SAME-DAY SHIPPING.
CROCS -R- US
TO: MELVIRA
THIS ↑ SIDE UP
WAIT!
MELVIRA, OUR VIEWERS ARE WONDERING, WHY DO ALL THIS BAD STUFF?
OH, WOW. WE'RE LIVE?
HELLO, TO ALL MY FANS!
LIVE STREAM
9
WELL, UMM . . . IT'S BECAUSE I HATE HEROES AND THEIR SUPERSNOBBISH ATTITUDES.
I WANT THEM TO SEE HOW TOUGH LIFE IS WITHOUT POWERS!
WAAAH!
I PROMISE NOT TO BE DEFINED BY MY POWERS ALONE!

I WON'T MAKE FUN OF PEOPLE AT THE GYM EVER AGAIN!
I PROMISE TO STOP SKIPPING THE LONG LINES AT THEME PARKS!
DEAR ME!
MY FOOT!
SNAP!
HELP!!!
IT LOOKS LIKE THIS IS THE END FOR OUR HEROES AND MAYOR POPSICLE.
IS THERE SOMEONE BRAVE ENOUGH TO SAVE US?
NO!
9

LOOK! IT'S A BUG!
IT'S A SQUIRREL!
NO, IT'S MISCHIEF!
COULD IT BE?
MY PROTÉGÉ TURNED ARCH NEMESIS?
OH, IT'S JUST ANOTHER VILLAIN.
WE'RE DOUBLE DOOMED!
NOT YET, SENIOR CITIZEN.
I AM HERE TO STOP MELVIRA!

ZOOM!
HI-YAH!
THUD!
SO, YOU FINALLY GOT THE GUTS TO SHOW YOURSELF!
SOMEONE NEEDS TO STOP YOU.
IT'S THANKS TO YOU I WAS ABLE TO SUCK THEIR POWERS!
HA! IF THERE'S ONE THING YOU'RE GOOD AT, IT'S SUCKING!
OH SNAP!
THAT WAS A GOOD BURN!

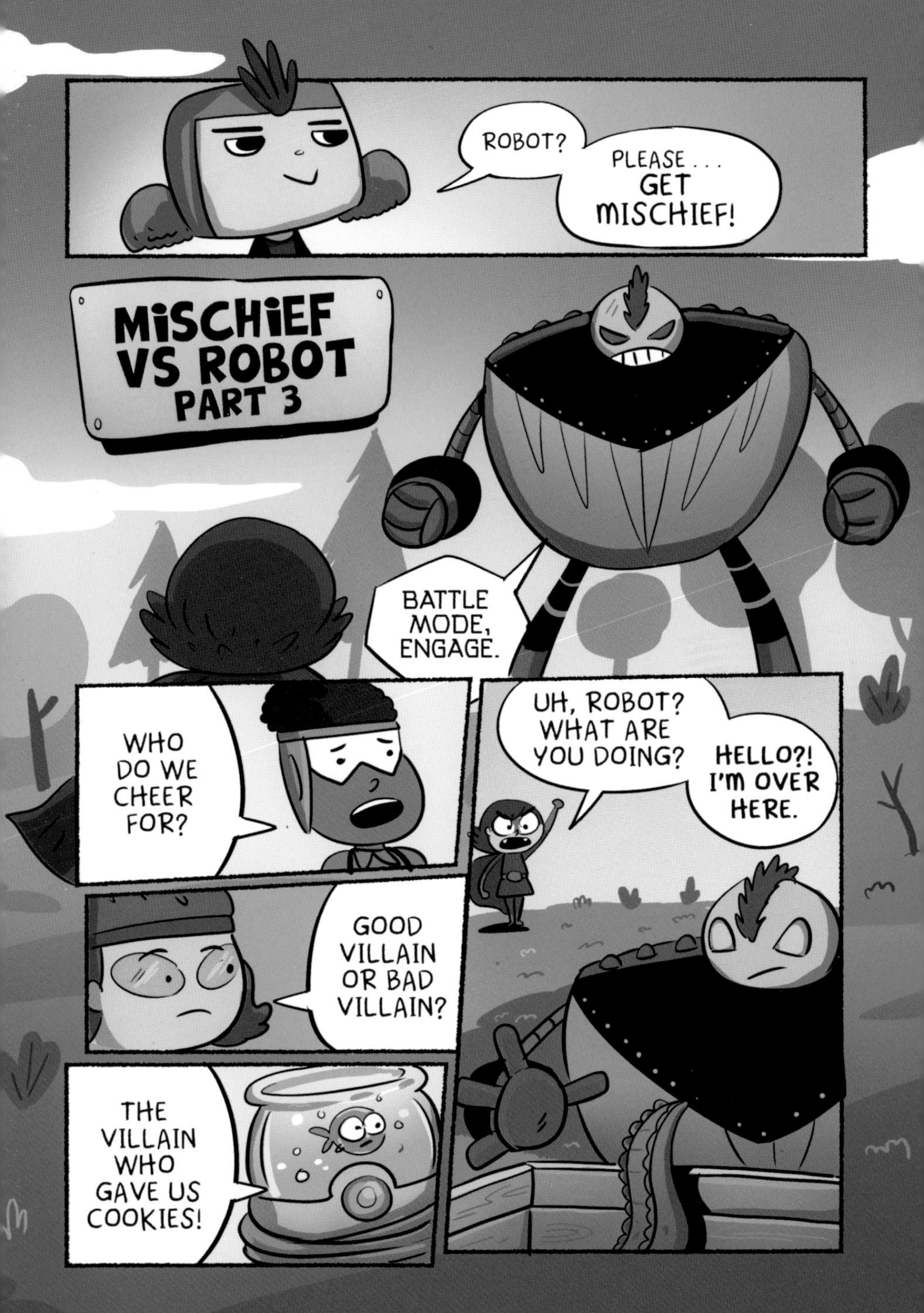
ROBOT?
PLEASE . . . GET MISCHIEF!
MISCHIEF VS ROBOT PART 3
BATTLE MODE, ENGAGE.
WHO DO WE CHEER FOR?
GOOD VILLAIN OR BAD VILLAIN?
THE VILLAIN WHO GAVE US COOKIES!
UH, ROBOT? WHAT ARE YOU DOING?
HELLO?! I'M OVER HERE.

CROC ATTACK!!
HOLY CROC A-MOLEEE!!!
POW!
WHERE'D THEY COME FROM?
CROCS-R-US!
AH!
THEY JUST KEEP COMING!

HI-YAH!
ROBOT CONFUSED. SEARCHING . . .
I SHOULD HAVE THOUGHT OF THIS SOONER.
LEFTY LOOSEY. HERE WE GO.
SCREW
SCREW
AHA!!
FOUND IT.
YET ANOTHER OFF BUTTON
ROBOT, SHE'S ON TOP OF YOU!

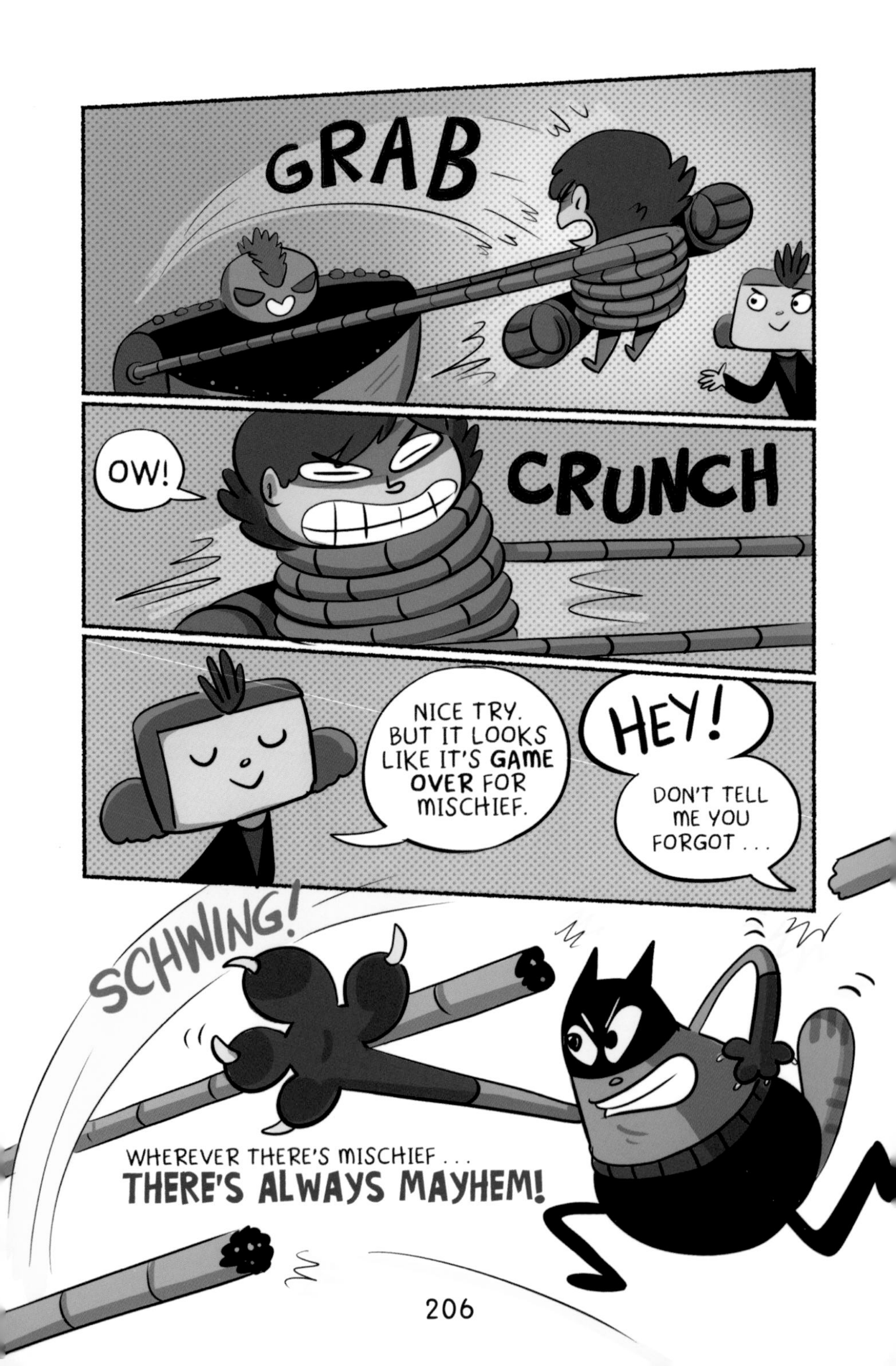
GRAB
OW!
CRUNCH
NICE TRY. BUT IT LOOKS LIKE IT'S GAME OVER FOR MISCHIEF.
HEY!
DON'T TELL ME YOU FORGOT . . .
SCHWING!
WHEREVER THERE'S MISCHIEF . . .
THERE'S ALWAYS MAYHEM!

AH! ROBOT!
ERROR!!! ROBOT DAMAGED!
THANKS, BUDDY.
LIKE I SAID, I'M YOUR SIDEKICK.
I GO WHERE YOU GO.
REVENGE MODE, ENGAGED.
MELVIRA, STOP!
I DON'T WANT TO KEEP FIGHTING.
BZZZTT.

I THOUGHT YOU WERE DIFFERENT.
BUT YOU BECAME EXACTLY WHAT YOU HATED.
HUH?
YOU SAID HEROES ACT BADLY BECAUSE OF THEIR POWERS.
YOU HAVE THE POWER NOW.
YOU'VE WON.
BUT IS THIS HOW YOU USE IT?
IS IT ALL FOR NOTHING?
SIGH
YOU'RE RIGHT.

BAWK!?
SHE'S RIGHT. I HAVE BEEN A BIG JERK.
I MADE A MISTAKE. I PUSHED YOU AWAY. I HURT YOU.
CAN YOU FORGIVE ME?
YOU REALLY MEAN THAT?
YES, I DO.
I'LL MAKE IT RIGHT. I PROMISE!
WHAT DO YOU SAY, "SISTERS IN TROUBLE"?
JUST LIKE OLD TIMES?
YOU CAN'T TRUST HER!
BAWK!

LADIES AND GENTS, IT LOOKS LIKE FRENEMIES MELVIRA AND MISCHIEF, SUPERVILLAINS EXTRAORDINARE, ARE ABOUT TO **JOIN FORCES.**
WHAT DOES THIS MEAN FOR US CITIZENS?
9
IF THEY JOIN FORCES, IT'S **GAME OVER** FOR US.
DON'T TRUST HER!
I ORDER YOU TO STOP THIS UNION!
I CAN'T WATCH.
SNAP!

CHAPTER 12

TP OVERLOAD

WHAT A RELIEF!
SO . . . YOU'RE GONNA LET US GO?
YEAH, ARE YOU GIVING BACK THEIR POWERS?
MY PLAN WAS ALL WRONG.
WE HAVE TO MAKE SURE THAT THOSE WHO ARE POWERLESS WILL NEVER FEEL THE WAY WE DID.
RIGHT.
AND THE ONLY WAY TO DO THAT IS TO DISINTEGRATE THEM!
EXACTLY!
WAIT . . .
WHAT?!

YEAH!
YOU GAVE ME THE IDEA.
I WAS JUST GONNA MAKE THEM **SUFFER**.
BUT THIS IS BETTER!
I DON'T THINK YOU UNDERSTOOD ME!
OH CRUD, **WE'RE DEAD.**
DEAR ME!
ALL THE SUPERPOWERS MADE THIS ZAPPER STRONG ENOUGH TO **DISINTEGRATE** ANYTHING!
BEEP
DESTROY MODE ENGAGED.
SCHWOOM!

KA-ZAP
AAAHHH!!!
MAYOR
LADIES AND GENTLEMEN, THE STATUE TURNED INTO ASHES!
BOO-HOO! MY BEAUTIFUL STATUE.
ACK!
MISCHIEF, DO SOMETHING!

BONK
BZZZZ.
IT'S BEEN SWELL KNOWING ALL OF YOU.
SEE YOU IN THE AFTERLIFE, DUDES.
FAREWELL, MY FRIENDS. WE'LL ALWAYS HAVE BOOT CAMP.
I'M TOO YOUNG TO DIE.
I'M THREE MINUTES YOUNGER THAN YOU.
ARE FISHES ALLOWED IN HEAVEN?

MELVIRA, WAIT! LET ME DO IT.
LET ME PROVE MY LOYALTY.
HERE.
HASTA LA VISTA, BABY!
BZZZT.
SNAP
SNAP

BYE, ZAPPER!
WHAT?!! MISCHIEF!!!
CHOMP!
KZZAT!
HI-YAH!
NO ONE HURTS MY SIDEKICK LIKE THAT.
POW
GLAD TO HAVE YOU BACK.
LET'S ROCK AND ROLL!

MISCHIEF AND MAYHEM VS EVERYONE!!!!
KROOM!
KROOM!
GET THEM!
POW
THWACK!
BOOM!
BOOM!

BAWK!
GET HIM!
WHOOSH!!
WHOA!
BAWKEEEE!
SMASH!

OW.
BONK!
YOU LEAVE ME NO CHOICE.
I'LL HAVE TO USE MY **SECRET WEAPON.**
THE TP SHOOTER 3000
CHOOM!
CHOOM!
YOU CAN'T STOP THE QUADRUPLE-PLY REINFORCED WITH ESSENTIAL OILS AND MINERALS.

ERROR.
YEAH!
ROBOT DISABLED.
THWAM!
GOOD JOB, MISCHIEF!
HEY! THAT'S CHEATING!
WHO USES TP AS A WEAPON?
I'M A VILLAIN
AND I'M SUPPOSED TO CHEAT!
TO GET SOMETHING DONE RIGHT, **YOU GOTTA DO IT YOURSELF.**

UH-OH.
THE TP SHOOTER IS **OUT OF TP**!
SPUTTER. SPUTTER.
I GUESS YOU'RE NOT MEANT TO BE SUPER AFTER ALL.
AH!
EEEK!
BITE!
STRETCH!
MY FACE!
HA!

SQUEEZE!
POW!
TICKLE!
SMASH!
ZOOP - ZIP - ZWOOSH!
MAYHEM?
MELVIRA?
WHAT THE HECK?!
GASP SHE COPIED ME!
NO!
SHE'S THE COPYCAT!
I'M THE REAL CAT!

WELL, THIS IS CONFUSING.
??
?
I'M THE REAL MAYHEM,
GET HER . . . SHE'S FAKE.
NO, I'M THE REAL ONE! DON'T BELIEVE HER LIES.
I HAVE AN IDEA.
PICKLED EGGS!!
WHOEVER CAN HANDLE ONE IS THE REAL MAYHEM.
I LOVE PICKLED BLACK EGGS.
YEAH! BEST SNACK EVER.
NOM NOM NOM.
SEE?

GURGLE
GRUMBLE
UH-OH.
BARF!
EWW!
ZOOP - ZIP - ZWOOSH!!!
BLECCH!
THAT WAS SO NASTY. I GIVE UP!
I GIVE UP!
OFFICERS, ARREST HER!
I NEVER THOUGHT I'D HEAR YOU SAY THAT.

I HATE YOU GUYS. YOU FOILED MY PLAN!
MOVE IT, VILLAIN!
BOOM! WE STOPPED HER.
HAPPY DANCE!
WE'RE AWESOME, WE'RE GREAT.
WOW.
MISCHIEF AND MAYHEM FINALLY STOPPED MELVIRA!
9
HELLO!
TOOT
HEY! WHAT ABOUT US?

OFFICER SNIPPY UNTIED US.
BUT WE'RE STILL POWERLESS!
CAN YOU HELP US?
DUDE
SNIP
HERE'S WHAT'S LEFT OF THE ZAPPER.
YIKES! LOOKS BAD.
DUD
I THINK IT'S TIME TO SHOW EVERYONE **YOUR SUPERPOWER.**
RIGHT!
SCREW
SCREW
TOK!
TOK!
ZIP ZIP

TA-DA!
USING MY BRAIN POWER, I REVERSED THE ZAPPER TO RETURN SUPER-POWERS.
WE GET IT. YOU'RE SMARTER THAN US.
LET'S TRY IT!
ZAP!!
IT'S WORKING!
BEEP
RAD!
YOU ROCK.
AND THE KEY TO THE CITY BELONGS TO THE HEROES OF THE DAY. . . .
YES!
WAIT! MELVIRA ESCAPED!
I GOT THIS!

MISCHIEF VS MELVIRA: THE CHASE!
HEY, COME BACK.
YOU'RE SUPPOSED TO BE IN JAIL OR SOMETHING!
IN YOUR DREAMS.
HUH? WHERE'D SHE GO?
MAIL
MAIL
OW!
MAI
KICK!
YOU'LL NEVER GET AWAY!
MAIL

DARN.
GONE AGAIN.
DO YOU MIND HELPING AN OLD LADY CROSS THE STREET?
OH!
SURE!
WAIT A SECOND. . . .
AHA!
YOINK!
WHY WOULD YOU DO THAT TO AN INNOCENT OLD LADY?
YOU'RE NOT AN OLD LADY!

HUFF-HUFF
I'M SO OUTTA SHAPE.
CAN'T BELIEVE SHE GOT AWAY AGAIN.
AH!
OOPS.
STOP! YOU KNOW I HATE RUNNING.
GIVE UP, MELVIRA.
THERE'S NO PLACE TO RUN.

WE COULD'VE BEEN GREAT TOGETHER.
WE COULD'VE FULFILLED OUR DESTINY AS SISTERS.
BUT YOU HAD TO BE THE GOOD KIND OF SUPERVILLAIN.
DON'T JUMP!
BYE, MISSY.
NO!

SOB
BAWK!
HA-HA!
YOU CAN'T GET RID OF ME THAT EASILY.

CHAPTER 13
FROM ZERO TO HERO!
THIS IS FOX, AT THE ANNUAL SUPER FESTIVAL.
IT'S BEEN A **LONG DAY**.
OUR WONDERFUL CITIZENS ARE HELPING CLEAN THE MESS . . .
AND THE HEROES HAVE THEIR POWERS BACK . . .
PSSHHH.

AND THE ROBOT IS ALSO GOING TO THE REPAIR SHOP.
FIX-A-BOT
WE HAVE A SPECIAL GUEST, MISS GRU WELLING, WHO CLAIMS TO KNOW MISCHIEF.
LET ME TAKE THAT.
YOINK!
WHEN I FIRST MET THIS CHILD, I SAW A SPARK!
I KNEW SHE HAD POTENTIAL.
I TAKE CREDIT FOR EVERY GOOD THING SHE DOES.
BUT HER CAT IS ANOTHER STORY. I'M HIGHLY ALLERGIC!
HELLO!
I AM IVAN. I ALSO KNOW THIS MISCHIEF AND MAYHEM.

FOR SAVING THE DAY, BIG CHEERS TO
MISCHIEF AND MAYHEM!
WE DID IT!
HOORAY!

WE'RE SORRY FOR NOT BELIEVING IN YOU.
YEAH. YOU ARE PRETTY AWESOME.
YOU KICKED VILLAIN BUTT!
WE WERE WONDERING . . .
WOULD YOU LIKE TO JOIN US?
DUD
WHOA!
JOIN THE LEAGUE OF HEROES?
HERO
WE'D BE HONORED.
AND YOU'D GET YOUR OWN SUPERHERO CERTIFICATE!
THIS IS WHAT YOU'VE **ALWAYS** WANTED.
HERO

SO . . . WHAT DO YOU SAY?
DUDE
WINK!
HERO
IT SOUNDS GREAT!
HERO
BUT MY PARTNER AND I ARE PERFECTLY HAPPY DOING OUR OWN THING.
ARE YOU SURE?
OH YEAH.
BESIDES, AS LONG AS THERE ARE SUPERHEROES AND SUPERVILLAINS . . . THERE WILL ALWAYS BE
MISCHIEF AND MAYHEM!
HERO

CHAPTER 14
A NEW PLAN IS HATCHED!
IN A REMOTE ISLAND VOLCANO . . .
I'M SERIOUS, CLAW.
I DON'T WANT TO HEAR IT.
BAWK!
I WOULD'VE LIKED AN EVIL-LOOKING LAIR, BUT THIS UNICORN ONE WAS A GOOD DEAL.
IT'S A TOUGH MARKET OUT THERE.

SURE, WE'LL NEED TO REPAINT THE WALLS.
AND THIS FLUFFY BED ISN'T WORKING FOR ME, EITHER.
AND WE'LL NEVER GO IN THIS ROOM EVER AGAIN.
POP!
BUT LOOK, AT LEAST WE HAVE A PING-PONG ROOM.

A NICE HOT TUB AND SPA.
AND WE HAVE AN INFINITE SUPPLY OF POWER . . .
THANKS TO THE VOLCANIC HEAT.
MEtube
webflix
hulo
PLAYS
BIRO
WI-FI INTERNET WITH STREAMING SHOWS.
SNACKS
SODA
AND A MULTITUDE OF VENDING MACHINES.

AND LOOK AT THAT PRETTY VIEW. . . .
C'MON, I KNOW YOU LIKE IT.
GRUMBLE

BUT THIS IS MY FAVORITE ROOM.
IT'S WHERE WE COOK UP OUR NEXT PLAN.
AND THIS TIME WE'LL HAVE LOTS OF HELP.
HA-HA!
I PRESENT TO YOU THE LEAGUE OF SUPERVILLAINS!
HA-HA!

* BUT WAIT, THERE'S MORE!

SUPER TOTALLY AWESOME BONUS SECTION

OH YEAH!
MAKE A SUPERHERO!
USE THE GUIDE TO DRAW YOUR SUPERHERO!
NAME:
AGE:
HERO NAME:
POWERS:
WEAKNESS:
HERO'S SECRET:

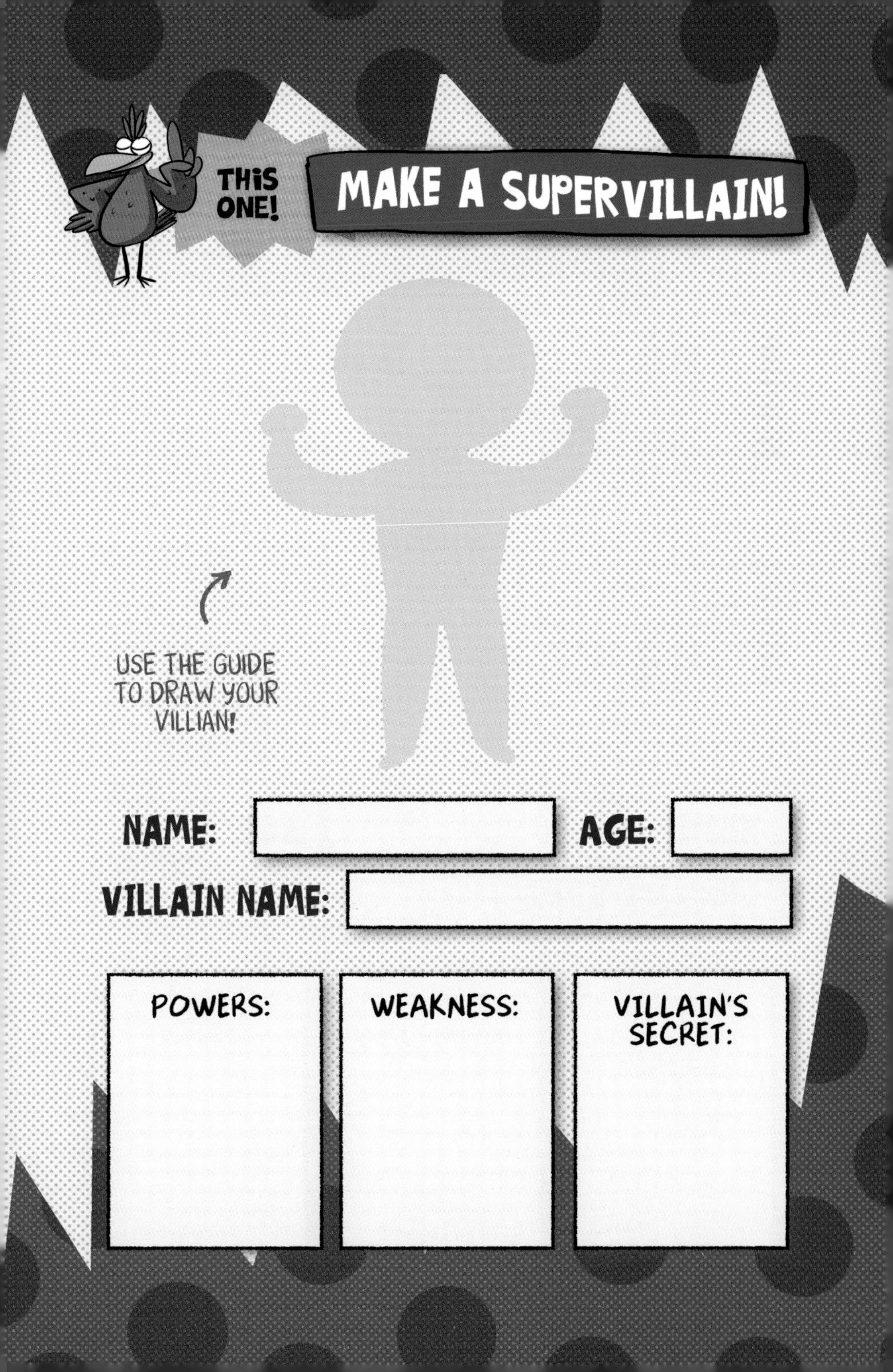
THIS ONE!
MAKE A SUPERVILLAIN!
USE THE GUIDE TO DRAW YOUR VILLIAN!
NAME:
AGE:
VILLAIN NAME:
POWERS:
WEAKNESS:
VILLAIN'S SECRET:

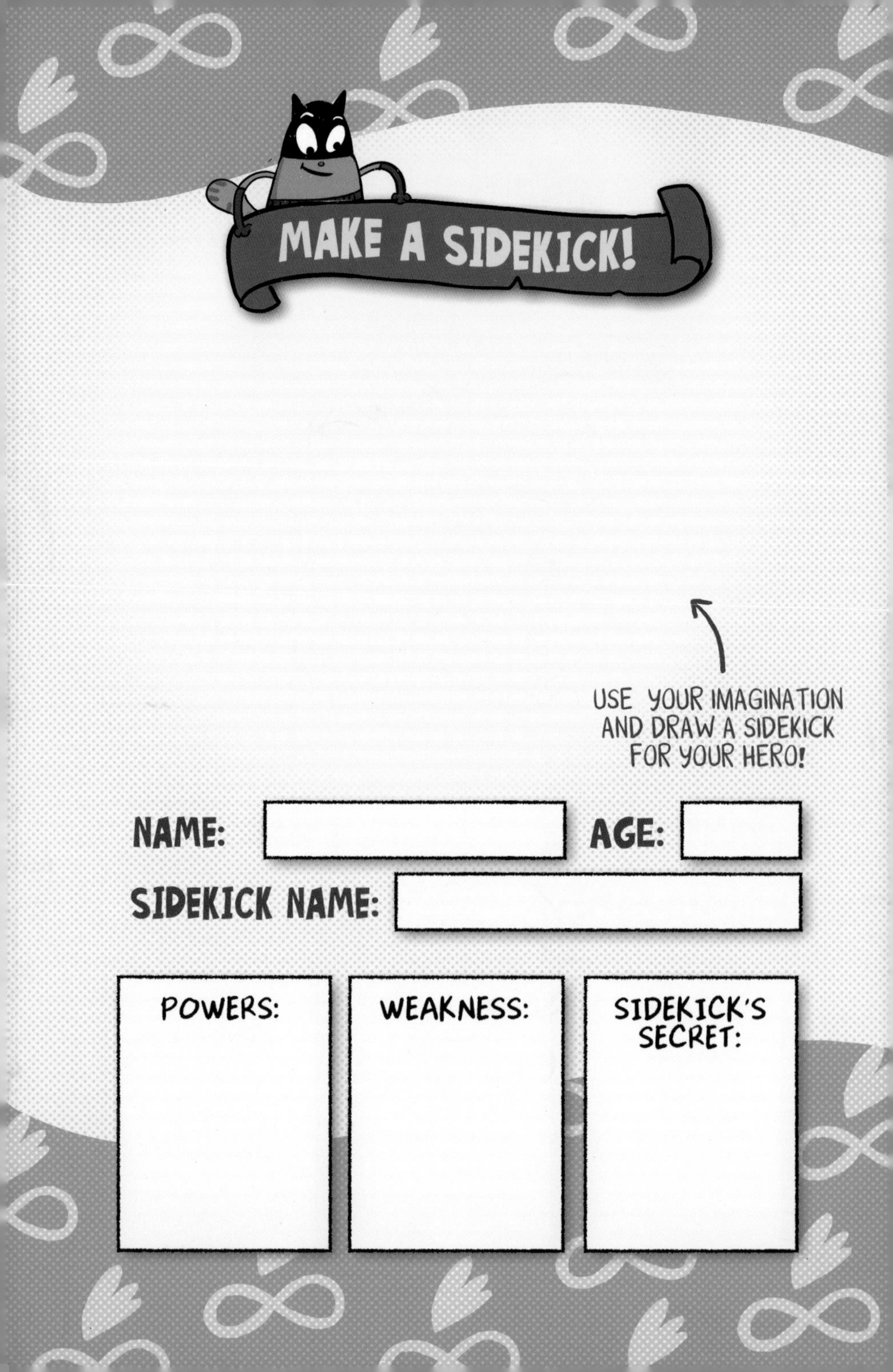
MAKE A SIDEKICK!
USE YOUR IMAGINATION AND DRAW A SIDEKICK FOR YOUR HERO!
NAME:
AGE:
SIDEKICK NAME:
POWERS:
WEAKNESS:
SIDEKICK'S SECRET:

MORE FUN!

DRAW MISCHIEF

THE SUPER-DUPER EASY WAY!

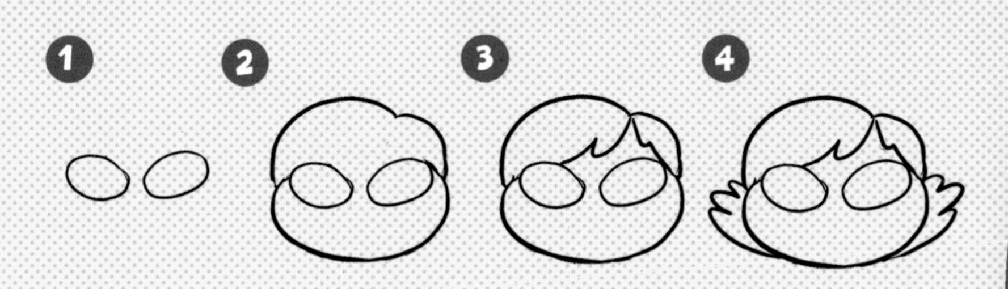

MORE BONUS!
DRAW MAYHEM
SUPERAWESOME TECHNIQUE!
1
2
3
4
5
6
7
8
9